ALLEN COUNTY PUBLIC LIBRARY

P9-ELH-263

AN OFFER OF MARRIAGE

"Andreas?" Amelia asked in disbelief.

He wore no coat, for it was a hot day, and his shirt-sleeves billowed in the breeze that tossed his golden curls. He carried some wildflowers in his hand.

He knelt at her feet and offered them to her.

"Thank you," she whispered, ashamed of the juice of ripe blackberries that still stained her hands from their picnic. She would have hidden them behind her back, but he reached out and grabbed one. He kissed it, then smiled and tasted the tip of one of her fingers.

"Your skin is as sweet as I remember," the count declared. He lowered his voice to an intimate whisper. "I adore the way you blush when I touch you, *carissima*. I must have you. Will you be mine?"

She averted her face in embarrassment.

"You are not asking me to be your mistress, are you? Because if you are, I—"

"Would you accept?" he interrupted.

Her basilisk stare gave him his answer.

"I thought not," he said with a soft laugh. "Forgive me for teasing you, beloved. I am very bad at this, for I have had little practice in asking ladies to marry me. . . ."

ROMANCE

Books by Kate Huntington

THE CAPTAIN'S COURTSHIP

THE LIEUTENANT'S LADY

LADY DIANA'S DARLINGS

MISTLETOE MAYHEM

A ROGUE FOR CHRISTMAS

THE MERCHANT PRINCE

Published by Zebra Books

THE
MERCHANT
PRINCE

Kate Huntington

ZEBRA BOOKS
Kensington Publishing Corp.
http://www.kensingtonbooks.com

ZEBRA BOOKS are published by

Kensington Publishing Corp.
850 Third Avenue
New York, NY 10022

Copyright © 2002 by Kathy Chwedyk

All rights reserved. No part of this book may be reproduced in any form or by any means without the prior written consent of the Publisher, excepting brief quotes used in reviews.

If you purchased this book without a cover you should be aware that this book is stolen property. It was reported as "unsold and destroyed" to the Publisher and neither the Author nor the Publisher has received any payment for this "stripped book."

All Kensington titles, imprints, and distributed lines are available at special quantity discounts for bulk purchases for sales promotion, premiums, fund-raising, educational or institutional use.

Special book excerpts or customized printings can also be created to fit specific needs. For details, write or phone the office of the Kensington Special Sales Manager: Kensington Publishing Corp., 850 Third Avenue, New York, NY 10022. Attn. Special Sales Department. Phone: 1-800-221-2647.

Zebra and the Z logo Reg. U.S. Pat. & TM Off.

First Printing: July 2002
10 9 8 7 6 5 4 3 2 1

Printed in the United States of America

This book is dedicated to my husband and inspiration for all blond heroes, Robert Chwedyk; to my loving and supportive sisters and brothers by birth and by marriage—Jane and Ed Hohe, John and Sharon Hoch, Joe and Linda Hoch, and Sonia and Ed Chwedyk; and to my nieces and nephews, who add so much amusement and exuberance to my life, Laura and Michelle Hohe, Sarah Hoch, Les Hoch, Danielle Hoch Shape, Eric and Matthew Chwedyk, Kelli Ebersole Dennis, and Cory Ebersole.

My life wouldn't be nearly as much fun without you.

Special thanks to the wonderful staff of the Algonquin Area Public Library, especially Craig Koukol for his invaluable aid in tracking down Napoleonic era military information for this book and finding me a good place in Paris to bury a certain troublesome corpse, and Vicky Tobias and Doris Botes, the house experts on Venice and Greece respectively. Any historical or geographical errors made in the actual execution of the book are, of course, mine alone.

One

Spring 1816
Paris, France

Seventeen-year-old Amelia Coomb's head ached from the strain of trying to communicate with the hired-carriage driver in his native tongue.

She was certain they had passed the same house on the same boulevard several times. They were going around in circles! Yet, the coachman did not understand or, as Amelia was beginning to suspect, he merely *pretended* not to understand her repeated requests that he ask one of the passersby for directions to the Cimetiére Père Lachaise. His manner from the moment she entered the carriage had been anything but respectful.

Tears of frustration welled in Amelia's eyes, but she would not give the perverse creature the satisfaction of shedding them. In truth, she had thought her tears all dried up after those first few weeks of hysterical weeping when she learned of Quentin's death. Certainly, she had been painfully dry-eyed until now.

It had been late winter when Amelia left England dressed in mourning for the man who had not lived long enough to make her a bride, and spring had come alive while she was on the sea. Yet the unfurling beauty all around her gave Amelia no comfort.

Amelia resented the first green shoots of spring and the fragrance of the sweet grasses that waved in the gentle breeze.

She resented the sun that shone so brightly upon her, indifferent to the great emptiness in her heart.

The light and warmth of that cruel sphere melted the merciful numbness that had encased her senses. It made her *feel* again, and feeling was excruciatingly painful to a young woman who had lost her one and only love.

She had come to France not to celebrate new life but to confront Quentin's death.

Instead of death, though, the small birds sang of life and hope; the flowers and the trees bore the sweet promise of innocent beauty.

And Amelia could not bear it.

"There—*there!*" Amelia called out from the carriage window. "That man! Ask *him!*"

Affecting deafness, the coachman drove on.

Not caring that she risked breaking her neck, the desperate Amelia pushed open the door and leapt to the ground while the carriage was still moving. Her crape-trimmed black bonnet fell off her head and hung around her neck by the ribbons.

"Monsieur! *Si'l vous plaît!*" she called out after the pedestrian, who turned to look at her in surprise. Amelia picked up her crushed bombazine skirts and ran up to him. It was undignified, but she didn't care. She blurted out the name of the cemetery she sought, and the man's pleasant expression hardened. His eyes took in her black clothes.

"*Anglais,*" the driver called out with an exaggerated shrug in explanation to the pedestrian after he had stopped the carriage and come to join them. The other man gave a short, ugly laugh. He rolled his eyes in derision.

And so the frustrated Amelia was left with *two* irritating Frenchmen to deal with instead of one.

Count Andreas Briccetti dismissed the hired carriage and strode along the delightful tree-lined Paris boulevard, glad for this respite from his native Venice, where he was treated with cloying deference in tribute to the five hundred years that the House of Briccetti had ruled its dominions on land and sea.

Today he was just another sea captain at liberty, although few of his fellow salts lived in a marble palace along the Grand Canal and owned a fleet of merchant ships that would put the armadas of several European countries to shame.

Andreas adored Paris. Even in the narrow back streets of the city inhabited by the poor, a refreshing vigor coexisted with the filth and violence. France had been defeated in the late war, but it was far from beaten. In Venice, to his sorrow, all was decadence and despair beneath its veneer of antique elegance.

Because of the agreements drawn up after the war, Austria owned Venice, and the Austrians were harsh taskmasters.

His beloved Venezia was a beautiful, once proud woman fading into old age and frailty, helpless in the grip of her Austrian oppressors, watching with sad eyes as her children were drained of hope and ambition and pride.

Not a pretty sight.

The count had earned the Austrians' trust with judiciously placed bribes and by pretending to cooperate with their subjugation of his country, so he was one of the few aristocratic citizens who could come and go as he wished—a privilege he exercised often. Andreas's faithful servants and his superficial friends looked askance at his habit of captaining his flagship personally on many of its journeys, but the count's amusing eccentricity was well known. His ship lay docked in Boulogne, the last stop on the return home from a voyage to America.

A drunken countryman jostled him as he passed by, and the count good-naturedly straightened the man and guided him on his way. His grandfather would have had the fellow flogged for such an offense against his august person. Andreas merely laughed.

For the moment, Andreas was happy just to be alone and unwatched.

In Venice, Andreas was on a perpetual stage, acting the part of the urbane courtier for the benefit of his watchdogs. His oppressors kept the movements of so rich and influential a citizen under close scrutiny.

Here he was anonymous. Or, at least, as anonymous as any man of such noble proportions and splendid physique could be.

Today he wore a black silk shirt with flowing sleeves and snug black pantaloons. Against the slight morning chill he had donned a black caped greatcoat. The ornate, jeweled crucifix given to one of his ancestors by the Doge of Venice was suspended from a heavy gold chain and lay against his breast.

Andreas took pleasure in the dashing figure reflected in the glass his valet had held for him.

His valet had lifted an eyebrow at Andreas's uncharacteristic choice of unrelieved black, but the count explained that this evening he would dine with his mentor and former tutor, Father Dominic Soranzo, ministering now to a convent of sisters east of the city, and it *was* Lent. Black seemed appropriate to the season of atonement.

3 1833 04277 7901

The valet, whose judgment in the all-important matter of fashion the count trusted implicitly, ventured to suggest that his master more closely resembled a pirate than a devout Christian, and Andreas modestly acknowledged that this was so.

After dining with Father Dominic, he would stroll the wide boulevards of Paris and select a café in which to partake of the excellent pastries for which Parisian chefs were famous. Perhaps he would call on one of several exquisite Parisian opera dancers who were eager to share Andreas's company when he happened to find himself in France.

Andreas stopped dead in his tracks when he heard the sound of an indignant feminine voice cut off by the unpleasant drone of rude male laughter.

A hired carriage was stopped at an odd angle in the street and partially blocked the road. This attracted loud protests from other drivers, while a young woman dressed in mourning argued with two Frenchmen, one of whom appeared to be the driver of the offending vehicle. The coachman was glaring at the girl, looking stubborn. She, looking equally stubborn to the point of tears, was addressing him in phrases of perfectly adequate English-schoolgirl French interspersed with English words when her vocabulary failed her. The other man rolled his eyes in comic derision at the girl for the benefit of a few passersby who had stopped to watch.

Andreas sighed.

After spending months confined to a ship with scores of contentious men to supervise, the last thing he expected to do on his first day of liberty was to embroil himself in a dispute among strangers.

But it was not in Andreas's nature to turn his back on a lady in distress, so he strode forward to enter the fray.

* * *

The stubborn coachman and the growing crowd of passersby just stared at Amelia in blockish imbecility when she repeated that she wished directions to Père Lachaise. She knew they understood her perfectly well. Even so, they shook their heads and gave her maddening smirks like nasty little boys intent upon pulling the wings off butterflies.

To her outrage, the coachman had the effrontery to insist that she pay him double the agreed-upon fare if she did not wish to be abandoned on the street.

She was about to let the coachman know what she thought of this blatant extortion, when a tall, imposing gentleman approached and gave Amelia's sneering tormentors a curt command to be silent. The spectators who had been enjoying Amelia's discomfiture wiped the smirks from their faces and dispersed.

The newcomer was dressed all in black from his broad shoulders to his polished boots, but his glorious mane of golden hair was bare. His brilliant blue eyes bored into the coachman, which made him shuffle his feet uneasily.

"If you will permit, madam," the gentleman said pleasantly to Amelia in lightly accented English. At her stunned nod, he addressed the coachman in short declarative French sentences. His expression had hardened to something quite alarming, and Amelia was glad it wasn't directed at *her*. Amelia, despite an expensively acquired finishing-school education that included careful—if mostly forgotten—instruction in the lingua franca of the polite world, could understand only one word in ten. By the time he was finished, the coachman's head was bowed and his shoulders sagged.

The coachman, after apparently having given her

champion the directions Amelia sought, got back upon the box of the carriage and started to drive away without her after all.

"Wait! Wait!" Amelia called after him.

"You must stop him," she said as she clutched the stranger's arm in appeal.

She stared as the abrupt movement dislodged an ornate gold cross studded with jewels on a heavy chain from its resting place inside the stranger's greatcoat.

He is a Roman priest, she realized with some surprise. That would account for the authority he commanded for such a young man and the fact that he was dressed all in black.

"Are you sure you wish it?" he asked, looking surprised. "He has been unforgivably rude to you."

"Yes!" she cried out. "Do not let him get away!"

"Fear not, little one," the man said reassuringly. He rapped out a command to the coachman, who stopped at once and leapt from his seat to let down the steps of the carriage with gratifying alacrity. "Will you permit me to escort you to the cemetery?"

Amelia's eyes burned. For a moment she could not speak. She was just so grateful. While her mother and a succession of governesses had been quite specific about the evils that could befall a foolish young woman who made the error of going off with a male who had not been properly introduced to her, surely this warning did not apply to a gentleman in Holy Orders.

"My poor child," he said softly. "Those men have distressed you."

"It is not their cruelty but your kindness that oversets me," she confessed. "Ever since Quentin died, I have not been . . . myself."

"You are certain you wish to go to this place?" he asked once they were seated in the carriage and he had given the signal to start. His eyes were filled with compassion.

"I must," she rasped. The lump in her throat was so painful, she could hardly get the words out. "Quentin's mother came with me from England, but she became unwell on the journey and is resting at the hotel with her maid to watch over her. I promised her I would find . . . him, and accompany her to the cemetery tomorrow."

The man leaned forward and covered her hand with his.

"You are a brave girl. Did you and your Quentin have children?"

"Children?" she asked in surprise. "Oh, you think we were married because of this." She indicated her crushed black bombazine skirts. "Quentin was my fiancé. When I learned of his death, I could not bear to wear colors. I still cannot. My mother quite despairs of me."

She gave a gusty sigh.

"She says it is well past time I put my sorrow behind me and attended parties again. But he was the husband of my heart. How could I do less than wear the full year of mourning for him?"

"Your regard for his memory does you both great honor," he observed. "He was a soldier, then?"

"Yes. A member of the Royal Tenth Hussars."

"Ah. A famous regiment, distinguished at Waterloo for bravery."

Most people became uncomfortable when Amelia mentioned her lost love in conversation, but not this man. It soothed her to talk about Quentin instead of bottling up her emotions tight for fear her friends and social acquaintances might think her morbid. This priest's parishioners must find his sensitivity of great comfort.

"Quentin had a part in that," she said, still fiercely proud of him. "He endured the cannon fire for days with his men, only to die in a duel with an embittered French officer while he was stationed in Boulogne with the occupation. He was on leave here in Paris when it happened."

"I am sorry," the priest said simply.

"Thank you." Suddenly too overcome with emotion to speak further, Amelia turned away to gaze out at the perfect sunny morning.

The cemetery, as it turned out, was far east of the city. There was a wall around it, but that did not hide its vastness from her, for the cemetery was high on a hill.

"Père Lachaise was built on the site of a famous estate," the priest said conversationally as he handed her down from the carriage.

"So that coachman knew perfectly well where it is," she said, glaring at the man, whose head was bowed slightly in what appeared to be embarrassment.

"The scoundrel!" she added indignantly.

"Perhaps he, too, has lost someone in the war," her companion said gently. Amelia felt rebuked.

A priest. Definitely. Or possibly a bishop from the look of the jeweled cross despite the fact that he looked not a day above five-and-twenty.

"You are right, of course," she agreed. "It is kind of you to trouble with my problems."

"It is my very great pleasure," he assured her.

He turned to the coachman and casually pressed a number of notes into his hand. The coachman's eyes grew wide when he looked at the face of the top note, and he dropped to his knees. He seized the priest's hand and kissed it. The priest accepted this homage stoically.

"You will wait," the priest said curtly in French after he had withdrawn his hand.

"Oui, monsieur," the coachman managed to croak.

The priest then took Amelia's arm and guided her through the arch at the entrance of the cemetery.

Amelia gasped at the majesty of the approach. Double rows of lemon trees lined the main path up the hill and were intersected a bit beyond the crest by a double row of chestnuts.

Her steps staggered to a horrified halt when she saw the mounded earth at the left of the entry that was unmistakably a series of communal graves.

She felt every drop of blood drain from her face. The priest reached out as if to steady her, but she waved him off. She would *not* faint.

"Edward said they put him in an individual grave," she whispered, referring to Lieutenant Edward Whittaker, Quentin's best friend and fellow officer who had acted as his second in the fateful duel. "He would not have said so if it were not true."

But he would if he thought the lie would give her and Quentin's mother comfort, and Amelia knew it.

"There are individual graves as well," the priest said, indicating the area to the right that revealed handsome funerary monuments interspersed picturesquely among the winding secondary paths and linden trees on up the hill.

"Yes," she said, feeling giddy. "His body must be in one of those."

Her escort took her arm and looked into her face with concern.

"Give me his full name and I will look for his grave. You may wait in the carriage, and I will come for you when I find it."

What a pathetic creature he must think her.

Amelia stiffened her spine.

"No, I thank you," she said. If Quentin could die in the service of his country, the least she could do is be brave and search for his grave herself.

Primroses and daffodils decorated some of the graves, and the sweetness of their perfume caused a lump to form in Amelia's throat as she searched the chiseled faces of the monuments for his name. It took a long time, for although there were not a great many graves, they were arranged randomly among the trees to suggest a sort of garden.

She had almost reached the end of a winding path high on the slope of the hill with the priest following at a respectful distance, when she came to a handsome white marble monument a little larger than those around it.

Lieutenant Quentin Lowell
Member of The Tenth,
The Prince Regent's Own,
Royal Regiment of Hussars
Born 1791; died 1815
He was the Bravest and the Best of Men

Amelia sank to her knees on the rounded soil and clutched in the dirt with her fingers. There were tendrils of grass on the grave.

"Quentin," she whispered. What hurt the most were those tender shoots of green, the new life that thrived in the soil.

He had been gone for so long. Long enough for grass to sprout over his grave.

Long enough for the marble to be streaked with the patina of neglect.

In her mind, she had carried a vision of Quentin, laughing. Now she would never again be able to think of him without remembering this grave and the cruel beauty of Paris in springtime.

Amelia let out a cry so loud, it hurt her throat. She rested her cheek against the dirt, glad for the sharpness of the small, hard stones abrading her skin.

"Poor little one," murmured the man in black as he raised her to her feet with gentle hands. Her eyes were closed, but she opened them when she felt his fingers fleetingly brush against her cheek, no doubt to dislodge some of the soil that clung there.

Amelia averted her face from his compassionate eyes and looked back toward the grave.

"I don't know how I shall bear it when I must go back to England and leave him here," she said.

He took both of her hands in a bracing grip.

"He will not be alone because those who love him will keep him alive in their hearts. And our loving Father will forever keep him in His care. Believe it."

"Loving," she said bitterly. "Quentin was four-and-twenty when he was killed. Do you call *that* loving?"

"It is not for us to question His ways but to trust in them. That is what we are told."

He held her hands firmly when she attempted to free herself and turn away from him.

"I am to *trust* that it is part of some beneficent heavenly plan for a good man to die in a foreign land and be buried among strangers," she spat out.

"No," he said wryly. "I said that is what we are told. We are mere mortals. Our minds and hearts are incapable of comprehending His plan."

"Can you honestly look at all the pain, all the *cruelty* that has been inflicted upon so many innocent people in this war and believe there is a *plan?*" she demanded. "All I know is my Quentin is dead." Her voice broke. "And the monster who perpetrated this outrage is alive and living in luxury in his island kingdom. *He* should be dead, not Quentin. He should be rotting in hell even as we speak, and I should be home, in England, planning our wedding."

She had never dared to speak such thoughts aloud. In England, hemmed all about by the expectations of Society, she would have been thought deranged or, worse, lacking in breeding. Her friends had petted and consoled her at first, but after the first shock was over they expected Amelia to put off the black clothes she had worn since that horrible day and go to balls again.

A lady of quality, her mother said firmly, did not rail against fate or strike out in fury or, indeed, weep very loudly.

Yet Amelia desperately wanted to strike out at something.

No. That was not it at all.

She wanted to strike *someone*. She wanted to make someone feel her wrath. She wanted someone to *pay!*

And here, thousands of miles away from everyone who knew her as a demure young lady, the only target for her rage was this patient man who looked at her with calm kindness. She realized he was accustomed to this—watching people suffer. It was a priest's responsibility to visit the bereaved souls under his jurisdiction to mouth empty platitudes at them.

Amelia clenched her fists. She deliberately clamped her lips shut to stop up the flow of words so bitter and so angry, she feared that to give them life would scorch the earth.

For a moment a red haze obscured her vision. She could not breathe.

Then she felt the man's hands grip her shoulders and shake her hard enough to make her teeth rattle.

"Let it out," he demanded. "Let the anger out before it chokes you."

Amelia's jaw hurt, and her throat was raw with the

effort of holding in the monster that battled to escape. If she let it, she feared nothing would ever be the same again.

She pushed against his chest in panic. She must escape from his presence before the monster freed itself to consume them both in a black bile of bitterness.

But her efforts were as a child's against his strength.

She managed to get a hand free and push hard enough against his chest to make him grunt in surprise. She took advantage of his slackened grip to deal him a ringing slap across the face.

In horror, she watched the angry print of her fingers darken his cheek.

Amelia brought both her hands up to her flaming face. How could she *do* such a thing after his kindness to her?

But instead of giving her the condemnation she so richly deserved, he placed a gentle hand beneath her chin and tilted her face up so she was forced to look into his eyes.

"Good," he said mildly.

Amelia's mouth dropped open.

"Good?" she repeated. *"Good?* Is that all you can say after I have made such a shocking spectacle of myself?"

"And on hallowed ground too," he said gravely.

He was right. This made her outburst so much worse. She was surprised the Almighty had not struck her dead.

She started to stammer an abject apology, but, incredibly, he smiled at her.

"It is good and right for you to express your anger," he said. "If left inside, it will grow and fester and poison your life. You are better now, yes?"

When she merely stared at him, dumbfounded, and

slowly shook her head in disbelief, he gave her a teasing smile.

"No? You may hit me again if you wish."

His smile was so infectious and his offer so absurd that Amelia felt the corners of her lips quirk up, just when she thought she would never smile again.

"That is better," he said approvingly.

Incredibly, they laughed together then, but her laugh sounded too high-pitched and giddy to her own ears. Helplessly, she felt her face crumple. Tears of reaction coursed down her cheeks, and she had no choice but to give in to them.

"Little wounded bird," the man murmured soothingly as he gathered her into his arms and allowed her to sob out her misery against his broad chest. She was shivering, and he drew the tails of his greatcoat around her for warmth.

It had been a long time since Amelia had been held in a man's strong arms. Only Quentin had touched her like this, and Lieutenant Edward Whittaker, their good friend, when he returned from the war to tell Amelia of Quentin's last days. It was comforting and alarming at the same time.

He smelled pleasantly of spices. Possibly incense, she thought vaguely. There was no new life associated with this fragrance in her mind. Only exotic climes and blessed oblivion.

When she ran out of strength to cry, she gently extricated herself. To her embarrassment, there was a damp blotch on his shirt. She felt sure that a lady of quality did not allow her nose to run all over a gentleman's person.

"I am so sorry," she began.

"Pray do not regard it," he said soothingly. "I have seen much sorrow." He handed her a handkerchief.

"Thank you, Father," she said gratefully as she blew her nose on it. It smelled of spices and *him*.

She looked up into his eyes, and surprised a startled expression in them.

"I am not of your faith. Is it presumptuous of me to call you Father?" she asked anxiously. "I did not mean to offend you."

"Father will do quite well," he said with a wry smile. "May I escort you back to your hotel now? You will want to rest."

Amelia shook her head.

"You are kind," she said, "but I would pray for his soul now that I have found him." She turned eyes of appeal up to him. "Will you pray with me?"

"Of course, my child," he said.

He bowed his head and closed his eyes; Amelia did the same. After several moments had passed, Amelia opened one eye. As if he could feel her looking at him, the man opened his eyes and lifted one eyebrow.

"Are you not going to . . . do something?" she asked.

A bit self-consciously, Amelia thought, he touched his forehead, his chest and each shoulder, then said something in an unfamiliar language she assumed was Latin. The capes of the black greatcoat flared out dramatically from his shoulders when he did so, and the sun set the jewels in his crucifix on fire.

"That is all, I think," she said as she gazed at the grave. She could not look away. Finally, the priest put his arm around her shoulders and drew her from the graveside.

"Thank you, Father . . . ?"

"Dominic," he supplied after a short hesitation. "Father Dominic Soranzo. I am on holiday from my parish in Venice."

"Father Dominic," she said with a smile. "You are

Italian, then. And I am Amelia Coomb. What must you think of me? Here I am, weeping all over you, and I hadn't even introduced myself."

"Much can be forgiven a soul in pain, my child," he said gravely. "It is not safe for a young woman of your nationality to travel alone here. The war may be over, but there is much bad feeling in France toward the English. May I escort you to your hotel? You are no doubt fatigued and hungry."

At that moment, Amelia's stomach growled. Loudly.

He chuckled, and she had to laugh. She broke off in consternation to find herself laughing for the second time practically over Quentin's dead body.

"He would have wanted you to laugh again," the man said, startling Amelia by reading her mind.

Impulsively, she grasped his hand and kissed the back of it, assuming from the coachman's example that in the Church of Rome one kisses the hand of a priest as a sign of respect. Her lips tingled from the contact of his warm skin.

"You have helped me so much," she said earnestly. "I do not know how I can ever repay you."

He looked startled and immediately drew his hand back as if to prevent further demonstrations of her regard. Amelia was afraid she had offended him.

"Seeing your smile was payment enough," he said kindly. Even so, he seemed somewhat discomposed, and Amelia was sorry for it.

Two

After a simple but satisfying meal of poached fish and fresh vegetables served in the Mother Superior's private dining room, Father Dominic Soranzo poured Andreas a glass of wine and regarded him quizzically from his bright old eyes. On ordinary days, the priest took his meals with the nuns and postulants in the common room, but Count Andreas Briccetti was an important guest and patron.

The Venetian nobleman paid the nuns handsomely to hide his former tutor from the Austrians after he spoke out so passionately against their harsh rule of Venice, he almost triggered the revolt prematurely that he and his illustrious co-conspirator hoped would one day free Venice from Austrian rule.

Father Dominic's residence at the convent was a satisfactory arrangement for all concerned. Thanks to Count Briccetti's largess, the sisters were able to build their much-needed new chapel before the old one fell down around their ears and acquired a middle-aged priest to say Mass in it daily. Father Dominic got a comfortable and undemanding situation that allowed him enough time at liberty to do charitable work among the poor and write letters to the members of the conspiracy that were then smuggled into Venice. And the count had the satisfaction of saving his friend

and mentor from martyrdom at the hands of the Austrians, a fate the old troublemaker had to admit he
would have been reluctant to embrace despite all his
righteous indignation for Venice's oppressors.

It was glorious to die for a cause but infinitely more
practical to avoid death and live to fight another day.
This is what Father Dominic had impressed upon his
most illustrious pupil from childhood, and Andreas
had learned the lesson well.

"You are quiet tonight, my son," Father Dominic
said. "What is troubling you?"

Andreas gave a long sigh.

"I regret that I am not good company."

"You are always good company. But I sense your
mind is somewhere else. Do you wish to talk about
it?"

"I met the most extraordinary girl today," said Andreas.

The priest's look of concern relaxed into a smile.

"Ah, is that all? You sly young pup! So you are
counting the moments until you can leave this boring
old man and rush into her arms."

"If only it were that simple," Andreas said ruefully.
"I have misled her about my situation in life."

"What? Does she believe you are a duke instead of
a count?" the priest joked as he raised the glass of
wine to his lips. "Or did you pretend to be even richer
than you are? How greedy *is* this young woman?"

"She is an angel," Andreas said glumly. "And she
thinks I am a priest."

Father Dominic choked on his wine.

"A priest!" he exclaimed. "Now, *there* is an unusual
ploy for attracting women. And is this strategy effective? I ask purely from an academic interest, you understand."

Andreas gave him a look of injured reproach.

"She is a lost little soul of an Englishwoman who came to Paris to find her fiancé's grave. Naturally I came to her assistance."

"Naturally. I assume this girl is very pretty?"

"Molto bella." Andreas kissed his fingers to the air. "And dressed in mourning for the past year, even though he died before they could marry. It argues for a loyal heart."

The priest looked chastened.

"Poor child," he said.

"She assumed I was a priest because of my black clothing and the cross I wear, and since she was distraught and in need of comfort, I did not correct her."

"Very noble," the priest said dryly. "I trust you did not distract the girl from her sorrow by demonstrating the skills for which you are renowned among the opera dancers of Paris."

Andreas gave him an injured look.

"For a priest, you have an evil mind," he said. "You should have seen me, mumbling over the fiancé's grave in Latin and mouthing platitudes about Our Loving Father and His Heavenly Plan to the poor girl. I sounded just like *you*. Then I escorted her to her hotel. I wished her well and gave her my blessing. It is a remarkable thing that I was not instantly struck dead. Then I came here."

The priest gave a snort of laughter.

"You do us proud, my son."

"A new experience, for certain," he agreed with an answering grin but sobered immediately. "She is all alone in Paris except for her fiancé's mother, who became ill on the journey and leaves the girl to her own devices. I fear for her."

"That is not good," the priest said. "There are many here who hate the English, and an unprotected girl would provide an easy target for their anger."

"Then Father Dominic must see to her safety," the count said with a sigh as he raised his glass of burgundy in a toast. "To the lovely Signorina Amelia and her broken heart."

"Father Dominic?" the priest said in surprise.

"Oh, did I not tell you? I gave her your name instead of mine." He gave the priest a sheepish look. "I could not give her my own, for she might recognize it."

"Of course. How tedious it must be to have every female of your acquaintance instantly fall in love with your handsome face and your fat purse," the priest jeered with affectionate contempt.

Andreas shrugged. It was true.

"Enough of this girl," Father Dominic said, putting down his wine and lowering his voice. "Is there heartening news from the Americans?"

"No," he said. "They have no taste for embroiling themselves in our fight for independence when they were at war with England so recently. I tried to appeal to their humanitarian sensibilities, and when that failed, I offered them gold from my personal fortune. They were not interested."

"Pity," said the priest with a sigh. "It may have to be the English after all."

"Perhaps, but I dare not approach them so soon after approaching the Americans. I can hardly march up to Whitehall with my proposal without the Austrians finding out about it." His tone grew bitter. "I must not give them any reason to doubt that I spend my days on shore in the arms of my many paramours, and my days upon the sea puking delicately into a silver basin."

The priest gave Andreas's shoulder a heartening squeeze.

"I know this is not easy for you, my son, for you

have the heart and strength of a lion. It is the role of a fox you play, to lull their suspicions."

Andreas's smile did not reach his eyes.

"It is the role of a buffoon," he said bitterly.

The priest raised his glass.

"And you play it masterfully, my son. What is a bit of humiliation now if the price is freedom for the country we both love? We must all make our sacrifices to such a glorious end."

"It is harder for you," Andreas acknowledged. "I may be forced to endure the embarrassment of being thought a fool, but I at least have the comfort of being able to live in the country of my birth if I choose."

"Someday I, too, will go home," Father Dominic said wistfully.

"Yes. I swear it will be so," Andreas declared. He made an expansive gesture toward the table. "Until that happy day, there is wine. There is good food and good company."

"And there are pretty English girls," the priest said with a teasing gleam in his eye.

It was just past two o'clock in the afternoon on a moody, overcast day pregnant with impending rain, when Amelia, Quentin's mother, and the elder lady's maid reached the cemetery. To Amelia's disappointment, no Father Dominic was waiting for them at the entrance. She had told the compassionate priest that Mrs. Lowell would visit her son's grave today, and she hoped he would come to give comfort to the bereaved mother.

It had been presumptuous of her to expect it of him. It was her place, and not his, to help Mrs. Lowell face the truth of her son's death.

Father Dominic owed her *nothing*. She was not even of his faith.

So, when Amelia and the maid supported the grieving mother's faltering steps to the place where Quentin lay, she was surprised to find the priest bending low over the grave and having an intense, low-voiced conversation with a grizzled man she assumed was some sort of cemetery caretaker. The Frenchman was kneeling beside the marble monument with a rag that moved listlessly in his hand and a pail of water at his side.

Even with her poor command of the language, Amelia could tell that the Frenchman was engaged in doing the priest's bidding reluctantly, and that he resented the priest's command that he clean the gravestone of an enemy of his country.

A lump grew in Amelia's throat. She had been too distraught yesterday to suspect that some of the yellowish stains had been made by those who resented the presence of a dead enemy officer in the garden of rest inhabited by so many French war heroes and took the opportunity to literally spit on the grave of a fallen enemy. How like the kind and compassionate Father Dominic to have the stone cleaned so Quentin's mother would not see it covered with the accumulated filth of neglect and insult.

Father Dominic turned his attention away from the Frenchman at Amelia's soft gasp to shake his disheveled golden curls out of his eyes and peer up at her.

The priest rose from his crouched position to stand before them. He had abandoned his coat in the heat of the day. Even so, he had an air of majesty about him.

"Oh, you dear man!" Amelia burst out as she threw her arms around him and gave him an ecstatic hug of gratitude.

The priest froze for a moment, but then he patted her shoulder blades rather awkwardly.

Amelia averted her eyes in embarrassment.

What was she thinking of?

He was a gentleman unrelated to her, and one who had taken a vow of celibacy besides. No doubt he was thoroughly repulsed by her familiar behavior.

But when she dared to look into his eyes, they held only kindness.

"You will forgive me," he said as he laid a gentle hand on her shoulder. "I am not accustomed to such heartfelt expressions of regard from young ladies."

"No, of course not," she murmured in mortification.

He reached to the ground toward his coat and retrieved the large bouquet of white lilies that had been lain protectively in its folds. He presented these with a charming formality to Quentin's mother.

"Mrs. Lowell, please accept my condolences on the death of your son," he said.

"I thank you, Father Dominic. Amelia told me of your great kindness to her, and I am most grateful," she said in a choked voice as she buried her face in the waxy white, fragrant blooms. Amelia's heart swelled. Mrs. Lowell's husband had soon followed her son to the grave, some said of a broken heart, and left his widow to grieve for both of them. The priest's sensitive and extravagant gesture was exactly right.

"Let me do this," Amelia said as she briskly stripped off her white gloves to hand them to Mrs. Lowell's maid and reached for the rag in the Frenchman's slackened grasp. She would have sunk to her knees in the soft earth, but the priest caught her arms just above the elbows to prevent her.

For a moment they were so close, she could feel his breath on her hair. His spicy scent mixed with earth and strong soap enveloped her.

"There is no need," he said gently. "This man has been paid to do his job, and he will do so or answer to me."

"I want to," she told him. "It would . . . help me to do this for Quentin."

The priest nodded and watched in silence as she knelt before the grave and scrubbed the cloth across the chiseled letters that spelled out Quentin's dear name. Tears of sorrow filled her eyes, but she felt comfort as well. In this simple task of tending her beloved's grave was a sort of healing.

When she was finished cleansing the white stone, she traced the name with a reverent fingertip. Just then, a single ray of sunshine burst from the cloudy sky and fell on her back and shoulders like the caress of a compassionate friend.

Amelia knew then that somewhere, somehow, Quentin's spirit existed still, and he knew she was there.

She rocked back on her heels and turned her face up to feel that blessed sunlight on her closed eyelids. No longer did its warmth seem cruel to her. When she took a deep breath and opened her eyes, the priest was leaning over her with one hand extended to help her to her feet. His eyes searched hers, so she smiled and nodded at him.

Father Dominic, who had reassumed his coat, prayed silently with the women. At the close of the prayer, Mrs. Lowell handed one of the lilies to Amelia, kept one for herself, and laid the rest across the mounded earth of her son's grave.

When Quentin's mother smiled at Amelia, she almost looked her true age. The year of bereavement for her son and husband had aged her a decade in appearance.

The Frenchman picked up the rag and the pail. The

other man dismissed him with a curt command and the caretaker shuffled away with his burdens.

As Mrs. Lowell looked back at the grave as if in farewell, Amelia drew the remaining man aside and tried to press some notes from her reticule into his hand.

He looked at them as if he had never seen money before.

"What is this?" he asked in surprise.

"Please accept it. For the lilies, and for whatever you paid that man."

"It was nothing," he said, putting one large hand out in an imperious gesture to indicate she should put her money away. "Please do not concern yourself."

"But I know the lilies were frightfully dear."

"A mere nothing, I assure you."

"Nonsense," she said firmly. "I am hardly destitute, and I *insist* upon discharging this debt."

"I do not recall the amount," he said in a voice that brooked no argument. "It is of no significance whatsoever."

"Very well, then, I accept your kindness with thanks," she said, "but this is not your responsibility. I am not of your faith, you know."

He gave her a dazzling smile. It was almost . . . flirtatious, but Amelia told herself at once that the thought was absurd.

"Perhaps I can convert you," he said.

She heard his stomach rumble and suspected that he had given away the price of his dinner in his magnificent gesture of kindness.

"Will you be our guest for dinner at the hotel tonight?" she asked, determined that he should not go hungry on their account.

"Please," she added when he said nothing. "Unless

you think dining with two English ladies would be damaging to your reputation."

She suspected that a priest, like any other member of the clergy, must take care not to attract unsavory gossip.

"My reputation?" he repeated with a quizzical smile. "No. I think my reputation can sustain the blow."

"Excellent," she said, relieved. "Then it is settled."

"I assure you," Count Briccetti said as the young Englishwoman pressed more of the unimaginatively prepared roasted chicken upon him, "I could not eat another morsel."

As it turned out, he dined alone with her. Mrs. Lowell, according to Miss Coomb, had fallen into a deep, healing slumber almost from the moment they had arrived at the hotel, and her maid had been reluctant to awaken her. The widow had slept poorly since they left England, and Miss Coomb was persuaded she needed rest more than she needed food.

To the count's mingled chagrin and amusement, he realized that the fair Amelia had the mistaken impression he was starving and destitute.

Andreas had not eaten so simple a meal in years. Even on board his flagship he had his French-trained chef to prepare the delicacies of which he was so fond. But he found the plain fare of chicken, potatoes, and limp vegetables delightful when shared with the lovely innocent.

Honor compelled him to tell her the truth—that he was a Venetian nobleman and merchant, not a churchman. But to do so now would be exceedingly awkward. She was smiling so trustingly at him. He could tell the bereaved Englishwoman had smiled little in the past year since her fiancé's death.

It was a new experience for him, this dining with a young lady who was obsessed with another man.

When the meal was at an end, Andreas absentmindedly reached for his money to pay for the dinner, but the girl insisted on paying.

Another new experience—most of the ladies of his acquaintance would not only have expected him to pay, but also would have spent the meal subtly hinting for a gift of jewelry or money as well.

It was odd and rather pleasant to have someone take care of *him* for a change.

"Take this, Father Dominic," she said, placing the remains of a loaf of bread and fruit into a napkin and wrapping it securely. She passed it across the table to him and at his look of inquiry added, "For your breakfast tomorrow morning."

"No, I thank you," he said, appalled by the thought of walking along the boulevard and into his luxury hotel with a napkin full of stale bread and overripe fruit tucked under his arm.

"I am persuaded the price of your lodging does not include food like this," she said earnestly.

"Yes, this is true," he acknowledged. And if it did, he probably would send his servant to complain at once.

Miss Coomb stood up and Andreas politely rose as well. She smiled up at him and he was struck again by how young and pretty she looked despite the austere black clothing. He would give much to see her golden hair freed of that depressing bonnet. She would be exquisite in ivory satin and gold tissue. Or, perhaps, in blue brocade.

"I thank you, Father Dominic, for all you have done," she said.

"It was my very great pleasure," he said. "Anyone would have done the same."

"You are a kind man and always see kindness in others," she said. "But I would have been quite friendless without you."

He took the hand that was offered and shook it firmly when he realized he had started to lift it to his lips. No priest of his acquaintance, he felt sure, would be caught in the impropriety of bestowing kisses on the knuckles of lovely young women.

How his friends would have laughed to see Andreas stand like a block because he wasn't sure how to respond to a woman who was perfectly content to end the evening before he wanted it to.

The evening had been so pleasant that Andreas almost made the very grave error of suggesting they continue it in his luxurious suite at the city's most expensive hotel, an accommodation that did not make it necessary for guests to smuggle their own breakfasts in from inferior inns.

When they parted company, Andreas walked along the street, feeling strangely reluctant to pursue his usual nocturnal pleasures. He was just handing the parcel of bread and fruit to the first beggar he encountered, when he heard a female voice call after him.

It was Miss Coomb, of course. No one else called him Father Dominic.

He froze, caught in the act of ungratefully disposing of the young lady's largess.

The girl glared at the beggar, who had already taken a big bite out of the bread. "You have given your breakfast away!"

The supposedly lame beggar immediately clutched the parcel to his chest and ran.

"Well!" she huffed, hands on hips.

"Forgive me," Andreas said, trying and failing not to laugh at her indignant expression. "I could not keep the bread when one of God's children had need of it."

"But he wasn't lame at all! He was just *pretending!*"

"This does not make him any less hungry," Andreas pointed out.

Her eyes melted.

"I do believe you are the kindest gentleman on earth," she said, "but now *you* will have no breakfast."

"Do not worry about me," he said. "I am amply provided for." This, at least, was not a lie, although he raised his eyes piously upward to suggest he was fed by supernatural aid. "Is something wrong? Do you require my assistance?"

"Wrong?" she asked, surprised.

"That you have come after me."

"Oh, yes!" she said. "Here is your handkerchief, which you so kindly lent me yesterday. I had the hotel staff launder it. And I thank you for its use." She traced the figure of a winged lion on the corner of the snowy linen. "Such exquisite embroidery."

"Yes. It was done by nuns," he said with a straight face.

"Well, this is farewell, then," she said hesitantly.

Andreas could see the regret in her eyes.

Poor lost little soul.

"When will you return to England?" he asked.

"We have bespoken passage in a week," she said. "We were not certain how long it would take to locate Quentin's grave."

"I am visiting Paris for a week myself," he said. Without thinking, he drew his thumb caressingly along the palm of her hand. "We could . . . meet."

She looked up quickly, and he drew his hand back as if hers had scorched it. He had forgotten again.

"At the cemetery, of course," he added hastily. "To pray for his soul."

"Of course," she said, looking relieved. "I knew that is what you meant."

"I'm sorry, of course," she stammered, confused.

"Don't be," she said, looking amused. "I know exactly what you think..."

Three

She dreamed about Father Dominic that night.

His smile.

His laughter.

His intuitive gift for knowing the trouble in her heart and saying precisely the right thing to comfort her.

Amelia's eyes flew open, and she sat up in bed. She put a hand to her pounding heart.

Since Quentin's death, the thought of accepting the caresses of another man had been utterly repugnant to her.

Until now.

Father Dominic was so different from every man she had ever known. The only time she felt truly alive was with him.

He would be shocked—utterly shocked—if he had any idea that her feelings for him were so personal.

She knew women in her neighborhood—spinsters and widows, mostly—who developed unrequited passions for the clerics who served them, and Amelia always was mildly embarrassed on their behalf. When they approached the curate as he stood greeting parishioners at the end of services, their faded cheeks would blossom into flame and their eyes would shine. Instead of merely shaking his hand and moving on like any sane person, they would find some pretext to bask a bit longer in his presence—a question, a comment on the sermon, or some observation designed to impress him with their piety or generosity.

The poor man would look self-conscious and his smile would stiffen.

But his fervent admirers would take no heed. In desperation to claim his regard, these afflicted women would persist in their inane compliments while their observers would look away in distaste or laugh behind their hands at them.

Amelia had long wondered how these foolish women could have so little pride.

Now she knew.

At least *they* had not centered their affections on a gentleman who had made a vow of celibacy.

If Amelia had any backbone at all, she would make some excuse never to see him again.

But to do so would be to deprive her reviving spirits of air and nourishment. Even now she felt her heart flutter at the idea of being with him.

Poor Quentin.

Amelia had loved him with all her heart. She had mourned him more sincerely than any true wife could have. Yet, when she was with Father Dominic, there were moments when she could not remember the precise color of Quentin's eyes. Or the sound of his voice.

With Father Dominic, there were moments when the leaden lump that had been her heart would beat for joy.

Yesterday she had actually stopped before a shop window to admire a blond straw bonnet with artificial roses along the brim and pink ribbons. Heaven help her, she had wanted—just for a moment—for him to see her in it.

Was she so shallow and disloyal a creature after all?

* * *

It was well past time for Andreas to return to Boulogne to collect his ship and his crew and return to Venice, yet he had lingered, idling along the wide boulevards lined with blossoming trees and flowers, nibbling pastries and drinking sweet tea with Amelia Coomb. More and more often they had been able to coax Mrs. Lowell out of her hotel room and into the light of that lovely Parisian spring.

Andreas should have been bored, squiring two proper English ladies about the city and visiting the cemetery to pray over the fallen lieutenant's grave with them. Instead, he was charmed.

He didn't know whether to be disappointed or relieved that it was about to come to an end.

He stood when Amelia came into the vestibule of the hotel to greet him.

She was still wearing black, but she looked far different from the tragic little girl he had met a week ago. Her face bloomed into radiance the moment she saw him. Her eyes shone with pleasure. There were no repressed tears in them now, and Andreas knew he was responsible for that.

What to do about Amelia was a question that plagued his nights, but not enough to tell her the truth and put an end to those lovely golden days spent in her company.

Now, it seemed, the decision had been made for him.

"Father Dominic, good morning," she said, holding out her hand to him. He took it in both of his. "Mrs. Lowell has a headache and will not be joining us today."

She looked pleased, and Andreas felt a burst of pleasure himself. Much as he pitied Mrs. Lowell the loss of her son, he treasured those days when he and Amelia were alone. If anyone had told him he would derive such ecstasy from strolling the Tuileries Gardens with a pretty young lady he was forbidden even to kiss, he would have hooted with laughter.

Instead, he wanted to howl with frustration.

"Is something wrong, Father?" Amelia asked, sensing his somber mood.

"I have received an urgent summons from Venice," he said. "I must leave tonight for Boulogne."

The brightness faded from her eyes. The pretty bloom left her cheeks.

"Of course," she said. "Your parishioners need you. Your holiday is at an end, and I have been selfish to monopolize your time in Paris."

"It has been a very great pleasure," he said. His lips tingled. He wanted very badly to kiss her. For propriety's sake, he would have to let go of her hand *now*. He did so, and stepped back to put some distance between them.

"I do not know what Mrs. Lowell and I would have done without your kindness and advice," she said as she removed her reticule from her wrist and withdrew a roll of bank notes. "Please accept this as a token of—"

"Absolutely not," he said, appalled by the thought of accepting money from her.

She had expected him to take the notes from her hand, and she was so flustered by his vehement refusal that she dropped them on the floor. He retrieved the notes and held them out to her. She took them after a small hesitation.

"Now I have offended you." Her eyes were huge with compassion. She thought the poor priest was too proud to accept her charity. "Please allow me to make this donation to your church. I am certain there are many worthy persons in your parish who would benefit from such a gift. I promise you, I can well afford it."

"I did not befriend you for money."

She pressed his hand.

"I know that. You befriended Mrs. Lowell and me out of kindness." Tears filled her eyes, and Andreas chided himself for the gratification this brought him. "I shall miss you. So much."

She would miss him.

Even though he had not bought her a single gift. Even though he had not flirted with her over caviar and champagne in the privacy of his luxurious suite. Even though she had no idea that marrying Andreas would bring his bride a title and a luxurious palace with which to impress her friends, she had fallen in love with him. The sweet girl was not experienced enough to hide this in the way of more sophisticated women.

If one of Andreas's ships had not gone missing off the coast of India and his presence were not required immediately in Venice to allay the concerns of his business associates and the missing men's families, he would probably invent an excuse to linger in Paris and enjoy Amelia's innocent company for another week.

And then another.

But all these stolen days must end just the same, with Amelia's going back to England eventually to bestow her radiant smiles on some fortunate young man of her own class and nationality, one who deserved them. One who could bring to her a whole heart.

Yes, it was just as well, for both of their sakes, that it would end now.

"This is farewell, then," she said, smiling bravely at him. She held out her hand again, and he took it.

Farewell. God be with you. Be happy, my dear child. His lips tried to form the words, but he was weak.

"I do not have to go just yet," he said, offering his arm. "But soon. We have time for a last morning walk in the gardens."

The Tuileries Gardens were designed by André le Nôtre, the greatest of French gardeners, under the patronage of Louis XIV, the Sun King, and they did both these luminaries honor.

The perfume of masses of daffodils and primroses sweetened the air, and the flowering trees sent a gentle rain of pink and white blossoms onto the green carpet below.

"It is all so beautiful," Amelia said, trying to sound cheerful even though she feared her heart might break.

"*Cara,*" her companion whispered in dismay when the effort finally became too much and she burst into tears. She felt him touch her shoulder, and she turned into his arms.

His body was stiff for a moment, but then he relaxed and caressed her back in gentle, soothing circles.

"It is all right, my child," he said.

It occurred to Amelia that he never said don't cry. Or, proper young ladies never feel this. Or do that.

Amelia knew she should make an effort to control herself, but his strong arms around her felt so good. She never wanted him to let her go.

She had loved two men in her life, and she would leave them both in Paris. Her first love, Lieutenant Quentin Lowell of the Prince Regent's Own, the Tenth Royal Hussars was dead. But Father Dominic Soranzo, the man she feared would be her last, was no less lost to her.

"I shall miss you so much," she sobbed.

He took one of those immaculate, beautifully embroidered handkerchiefs from his pocket and dried her eyes with it. She took it from his hand, turned her back to him, and blew her nose. The linen smelled subtly of the spicy fragrance she would always associate with him.

"I shall miss you as well," he said.

"I have never known a man so noble or generous," she said, turning to face him.

"I am neither," Father Dominic said in an oddly choked voice. "Far from it."

"You are," Amelia said, smiling. "You have given me the most precious gift of all—the will to live."

"You always had that," he said, pressing her hand. "Come, sit down."

She sank to a little stone bench in a pretty alcove of trees. He crouched down before her and framed her face with his hands.

"You are all right?" he asked in concern. She nodded. "This has been a sad journey for you, but you are strong. You will endure if you will have faith."

"Oh, Father Dominic," she said, falling forward into his arms to rest her head upon on his shoulder. "I am not strong. Not strong at all. I thought I was, but—"

He held her tightly for a moment before he relaxed his hold so he could look into her face. Then, as if he could not help himself, he kissed her.

Amelia's world fell away until there was nothing left but his arms supporting her and his mouth on hers. Enveloped in his warmth and scent, she gave a sob of surrender.

"No, this is wrong," he said as he wrenched his lips away from hers.

His hands lingered at her waist for a moment as he very carefully set her back on the bench, and then he stood up. She rose to her feet at once, but he had turned his back to her.

"Please, give me a moment," he said in a choked voice when she touched his shoulder.

How she must have shocked him, throwing herself at him like that!

Amelia wanted to die of mortification.

"I am sorry," she said as renewed tears ran down her cheeks. "So sorry. Oh, what must you think of me?"

"The fault is mine. *Entirely* mine," he said, turning to face her. It was so like him to shoulder the blame. "Amelia—"

He had taken vows; she did not share his faith, but simple decency demanded that she respect those vows. Yet she had practically *begged* him to kiss her. And now he had lost all respect for her.

Amelia could not bear to hear him say that what had happened between them was a sin, and she must never think of him again.

She knew she could not promise him that.

She pressed her hands to her flaming cheeks and fled from his presence. "Amelia!" he called after her, but she did not stop. She waved to the driver of a hired carriage as soon as she was on the street outside the gardens.

"Amelia!"

She looked back to see him standing at the edge of the tree-lined boulevard, breathing hard. He reached his hand out toward her.

"Farewell!" she cried, and leapt into the carriage. She wept softly into his handkerchief all the way back to her hotel.

He had frightened her badly.

Count Andreas Briccetti, he reflected ironically, certainly had lost his touch with the ladies. The poor girl had run from him as if all the devils of hell were chasing her.

It was just as well. He had been on the point of telling her the truth—that he was not the saintly priest she thought she knew, but a pathetic liar who burned for her.

Even now he thought about pursuing her to her hotel to confess the truth and beg forgiveness for deceiving her and Mrs. Lowell.

And then what?

She would despise him, of course. How could she not?

No. He would do the noble thing. For a little while, with her, he was not the vain, manipulative, deceitful creature he had become but the good and honorable man God had intended him to be.

For her sake, let him be that man awhile longer.

Andreas gave a sigh of resignation and returned to his hotel to collect his valet and his baggage as he prepared to return to his empty, luxurious life.

Mercifully, Amelia and Mrs. Lowell's crossing back to England was a peaceful one.

"Mother!" Amelia cried out with pleasure when the post chaise let down its passengers at the appointed inn in Brighton. She had put Quentin's mother and the maid aboard a stagecoach in Dover for the last leg of their journey home and parted company with them.

"My darling!" Mrs. Coomb's cheeks were bright with tears of relief. "How I worried about you."

Amelia embraced her mother.

"I am well, Mother," she said cheerfully. "How nice you look. How did you know I would arrive today?"

"I have come here every day since I received your letter. Oh, Amelia. All I want is for you to be happy!"

"And so I shall, dearest," Amelia said soothingly.

Mrs. Coomb stood back to look into her daughter's face. She touched her cheek.

"You look wonderful," she marveled. "And I was so afraid seeking Lieutenant Lowell's grave would send you into a decline."

"It was something I had to do to put his death behind me, and I feel better now. In fact, I have decided to leave off my mourning," Amelia said, knowing nothing would delight her mother more.

"It is a miracle," Mrs. Coomb exclaimed.

Amelia smiled fondly at her mother. No doubt that good lady was already planning Amelia's trousseau.

Why spoil her happiness by telling her the truth—that there would be no wedding bells for Amelia.

Not now. Not ever.

Quentin was at peace and so, in a way, was she.

Amelia had loved and lost twice now, but she had spent enough time in self-indulgent grieving.

If Father Dominic could reject the comforts of a spouse and family to dedicate himself to good works, so could she.

She would never see his face again or hear his voice, but she could, in this way, share his life. There was joy in helping others. He had taught her that.

It would be enough; it would have to be.

For how could she fall in love with an ordinary man once she had known a saint?

Four

Spring 1820
London

Lady Madelyn Langtry's lovely face lit up when she saw Amelia in the reception line. The candlelight turned the noblewoman's bright hair the color of burnished flame and danced along the glittering emeralds at her throat. Her low-cut gown was fashioned of white and gold tissue.

"Miss Coomb," Lady Madelyn exclaimed, touching her powdered cheek to Amelia's. "How beautiful you look!"

"Yes, all the mud washed off after all," Amelia said as she smoothed the skirt of a yellow evening gown kissed with white lace at the neckline and sleeves. Matching yellow ribbons were entwined through the bouquet of curls at the nape of her neck.

Lady Madelyn laughed merrily.

The ladies had struck up an acquaintance at the school Lady Madelyn sponsored for the indigent in Cheapside after Amelia, a volunteer instructress at the school, had gotten all muddy extracting two small, pugnacious boys from where they were writhing and pounding each other in a mud puddle, much to the disappointment of the cheering crowd of boys surrounding them.

Lady Madelyn was being guided through the facility by the headmaster at the time, and that good man had nearly expired from embarrassment when he and his patroness came upon this vulgar scene. He had been telling her how his regimen of studies had produced industrious, well-behaved little boys.

The earl's daughter, instead of being shocked and displeased, simply held out a dainty, gloved hand to Amelia and took her off with her to her town house in Grosvenor Square to help her wash away the mud. By the time the ladies had enjoyed a pleasant discussion about repairs for the school over tea and scrumptious little cakes, they had become fast friends.

Amelia's mother had been ecstatic when they received the elegant ivory vellum invitation trimmed in gold leaf. Lady Madelyn's balls were very exclusive, and Mrs. Coomb was certain that the guest list had to be filled to bursting with eligible young men capable of winning Amelia's obstinate heart.

Mrs. Coomb almost despaired of holding a grandchild in her arms, for while Amelia had left off mourning for her dead fiancé four years ago, she had turned down every one of the proposals from perfectly acceptable gentlemen she had received in the ensuing years.

So her spirits rose when Lady Madelyn pressed Amelia's hand and said, "There are several gentlemen I am determined you shall meet, my dear. I shall introduce them to you as soon as I can break away from here."

"How kind," Amelia murmured. "Of course, I shall be delighted to meet your friends."

"So pleased you could join us, Mrs. Coomb," Lady Madelyn said as she pressed that gratified lady's hand.

Mrs. Coomb could have kissed her.

But it turned out to be an evening like any other. Amelia danced with all the young men to whom Lady Madelyn introduced her with every appearance of pleasure, but later, when Mrs. Coomb delicately questioned her on whether any had attracted her particular attention, she could not recall any of their names.

"Mama, there is plenty of time to think of *that*," Amelia said with an airy wave of her hand toward Lady Madelyn, who was approaching them.

Mrs. Coomb perked up. If Amelia would not listen to her mother, she *might* listen to a worldly young matron whose wide acquaintance included the very cream of society. With Lady Madelyn was her husband, Mr. Robert Langtry. Better and better. Lady Madelyn and her spouse by all accounts were deliriously happy in their marriage. And there was no one more dedicated to marrying off all her friends than a happily married woman.

"What shall we do with my Amelia?" Mrs. Coomb asked Lady Madelyn on impulse. "There is no man in England she can be persuaded to marry."

"She is waiting for the right one, like I did, of course," Lady Madelyn said with a look of absolute adoration at her husband. In answer, he gave her shoulders a playful little squeeze and smiled down into her eyes. "Oh!" she added archly. "Did you think I meant *you*, Robert?"

"I *know* you did," he said. "I'm off to see the children to bed, love. Don't run away with any cavalry officers in my absence."

Lady Madelyn pursed her lips in a pretend kiss for his benefit as he sauntered off, a gentleman well convinced of his wife's devotion.

Mrs. Coomb sighed. She really couldn't help it. She *so* wanted her cherished daughter to find happiness, and nothing Amelia said would convince her that a spinster of one-and-twenty found happiness by teaching grubby little boys in a charity school and collecting discarded clothes for the poor.

"Well, we must see what we can do to find a gentleman who meets Amelia's high standards," said Lady Madelyn. Her eyes were sparkling with mischief.

"Traitoress!" But Amelia was smiling.

"Perhaps a continental gentleman," Lady Madelyn continued. "With a title, of course. How should you like being a baroness or a countess?"

"That would be very pleasant." But Amelia was just humoring Lady Madelyn. She took the same noncommittal tone with her mother when she tried to interest her in this gentleman or that. Mrs. Coomb didn't know what she was going to do with the provoking girl!

"Robert and I are going to Europe soon, Amelia," Lady Madelyn said, "on some unofficial business with the diplomatic service. We should be delighted to have your company."

Mrs. Coomb held her breath.

It would be just the thing to get Amelia away from all her tiresome little charities and into the mainstream of continental society.

But Amelia was already shaking her head.

"You are very kind, Lady Madelyn, but my obligations with the school—"

"Please reconsider," Lady Madelyn coaxed. "There is no sight more beautiful in all the world as Venice at sunset."

Amelia jolted like a fish on the hook.

"Venice?" she repeated, looking positively enthralled.

Mrs. Coomb said a silent prayer of thanksgiving.

"Yes," Lady Madelyn confirmed. "You will adore Venice. Do come."

"Venice," Amelia said again. "Yes, Lady Madelyn. I should be very pleased to see Venice."

"Cruel beauty," declaimed Mr. William Whittaker in theatrical tones. He was the brother of Quentin's friend, Lieutenant Edward Whittaker, and could always be relied upon to ask her for a dance whenever they found each other at the same ball. "I have been paying charming compliments to you for the past quarter hour and you have not heard a one. I think I shall go forth at once and put a period to my existence."

Amelia rolled her eyes.

"Of course I am paying attention, Mr. Whittaker. You know there is nothing I enjoy more than driving you mad from unrequited passion."

It was an old joke between them.

He had first asked Amelia to marry him two years earlier under duress from his mother, who was pressuring him to find a healthy, well-dowered girl to get heirs upon, and Amelia knew that for all his protestations to the contrary, he would be taken aback if she suddenly decided to accept him.

Mr. Whittaker quite relished being a bachelor if half the tales of his amorous exploits circulating in London were to be believed. His overbearing mother had been at him again, Amelia suspected. Otherwise, he would not have come anywhere near so respectable an entertainment as Lady Madelyn's ball.

Marriage-obsessed mothers were something they had in common, so they understood each other quite well.

"I suppose you particularly liked the part where I compared your earlobes to the most delicate of sows' ears."

"You caught me," she admitted with a rueful smile. "Forgive me, dear friend. I have much on my mind."

"You cannot mean to abandon me now," he said when the dance ended and Amelia moved out of his arms.

"I am a cruel beauty, remember?" she said over her shoulder as she prepared to leave him.

"May I fetch you some punch?"

"No, Mr. Whittaker, I thank you. Enjoy your evening."

He gave a long, dispirited sigh.

"Someday when you are looking down on my cold, dead face—"

"I will know that some jealous husband finally has caught up with you," she said as she walked away.

To her satisfaction, his laughter followed her. She would not hurt his feelings for the world, but she desperately needed to be alone. Smiling mechanically, she left the ballroom and found a little salon where she could let down her guard at last.

She pressed her shaking hands to her flushed cheeks.

Venice.

It was irresistible.

Four years later she remembered every expression on Father Dominic's handsome face. She heard his voice in her dreams.

And she could still feel his lips on hers. She relived his kiss, over and over, through the years. She could taste his hunger, and her own.

What would happen when she saw him again?

Would he even remember her name?

Amelia had made a fool of herself when they parted in Paris, but she was no longer a sad, unhappy, vulnerable girl.

A wise woman would stay far away from Venice, but she, it seemed, was not a wise woman.

She wanted to see him again.

She *needed* to see him again.

She would be cool. Dignified. Gracious. She would tell him about her charity work in London so he would know how much meeting him had changed her life.

She would thank him for taking care of her and Mrs. Lowell in Paris and insist upon making a generous donation to aid him in his work. She had come into her fortune with her twentieth birthday, and she could well afford it.

Perhaps then she could assuage the guilt that still haunted her for that wonderful, shameful kiss.

Father Dominic was a man of God, a man so noble that it had been a grave impertinence for her to want him for herself.

But that was in the past.

Amelia understood at last the commitment of a person who dedicated his life to serving mankind, for that is what she had done herself.

She and Father Dominic could never be lovers—not on this earthly plane—but they could be friends and equals.

The afternoon of their arrival in Venice, Amelia and Lady Madelyn were walking along the Grand Canal, browsing in the charming little shops that lined the Rialto Bridge. Lady Madelyn's husband followed with his elder niece and nephew, delightful young people who had accompanied them on the journey. Two younger children were at the embassy with their governess and small staff of nursemaids. In Lady Madelyn's opinion, one was never too young to acquire that desirable if illusive quality known as town bronze.

"My dear, I hope you will be all right on your own today," Lady Madelyn said to Amelia. "I feel like a *wretch* for deserting you on our first day in Venice, but I absolutely cannot get out of this appointment. I am here in a purely unofficial capacity, of course, but Whitehall is counting on me to smooth over some awkwardness between a prominent British citizen and the Austrian authorities here. They have detained the poor man for some impropriety, and his family is quite distressed over the affair."

"I understand completely, Lady Madelyn," Amelia assured her.

"Such a pity that you have no acquaintance in Venice—oh, Amelia!" She stopped before the display window of a millinery shop. "What a *darling* bonnet. It would look ravishing on you! Do let us go in so you can try it on."

"It is very pretty, but I have quite enough bonnets, so we needn't bother. Actually, I did meet someone from Venice a few years ago," Amelia said, trying to hide her elation. She had spent most of the voyage rehearsing excuses to rid herself of her friend's company for a day so she could seek out Father Dominic. She wouldn't even have to lie. Much. "Perhaps today I will seek out . . . her direction."

"Are you sure, Miss Coomb?" Mr. Langtry asked. "I am taking Mark and Melanie to the Piazza San Marco in order to tour the basilica. We should be quite charmed to have you join us."

"I would not dream of intruding on your family outing," Amelia said quickly. "I am eager to see my old friend, I promise you."

"As you wish, then," Lady Madelyn said, relieved. "We will make it up to you for being such negligent hosts, won't we, Robert? Count Briccetti has invited us to a masquerade ball at his palace tonight."

"That sounds delightful," Amelia said distractedly. She could not care less about some frivolous masquerade ball.

Amelia was in Venice at last.

And today she might see *him*.

It was all Amelia could do to hide her impatience for Lady Madelyn to be on her way to her appointment so Amelia could begin her systematic search of all the churches in Venice for the compassionate man who had given her the courage to live all those years ago.

It was almost sunset when she found him.

She spent the entire day going from one church to the other by gondola or by foot.

At last her search took her to a small, pretty island and a jewellike church in the Byzantine style. Fortunately, Amelia's Italian was much more proficient than her French, and she understood the priest who approached her quite well.

Father Dominic Soranzo had served at the church, the priest confirmed, but he was dead this past year of a fever contracted while he was caring for the poor.

How like him, Amelia thought.

"I met him several years ago in Paris," Amelia said as she fought tears. "Such a kind man. He was of great consolation to me at a very sad time in my life."

"His death was a loss to us all," the priest said. "You are pale. Are you ill, signorina? May I bring you a glass of water?"

"No, I thank you," she said, forcing a smile. Father Dominic would want her to be brave. "It is just such a shock to learn of his death. He was so young."

"Young?" the man repeated, looking surprised. "It

is true that he was young in his heart. He kept his sense of humor until the day he died."

Of course, Amelia thought with a fleeting smile. He would.

"Where is he buried?" Amelia asked.

"In our little garden outside the gate behind the church. It was his favorite place."

Now, Amelia reflected sadly, her friendship with Father Dominic had come full circle. It began in Paris over Quentin's grave; now it would end in Venice over his.

"Will you show me where he . . . rests?"

"This way, signorina."

It was so simple. Just a white stone with his name and a cross and some stylized floral decorations chiseled on it. There were flowers planted around the slightly mounded earth.

She might have expected that his grave would be well tended by those who knew and loved him.

But I am not here, she could almost hear him saying in her mind. No more than Quentin's soaring spirit was confined by that sad grave in Paris.

To properly mourn Father Dominic, Amelia went back into the cool church and knelt in one of the pews until her knees were stiff, even though so pure a soul hardly needed her prayers.

She spent an hour on her knees thanking the Almighty for sending Father Dominic to her at her time of need. Once more she dedicated her life to carrying on the work that he had begun. She would follow his example by serving others.

Then she stood and squared her shoulders.

He would want her to laugh again. He would want her to serve joyously, for life is a gift that must not be squandered.

Father Dominic had taught her that.

She would dress in her most beautiful gown tonight and go to the masquerade ball. There she would honor his memory by celebrating his life instead of mourning his death.

Five

The face of Amelia's maid was radiant with satisfaction as she dressed her mistress's hair in upswept curls and set a handful of tiny diamond-studded combs seemingly at random among them.

"I was afraid you would never wear it, miss," the maid said as she regarded the sumptuous rose brocade gown Amelia's mother had insisted she purchase before she left London. "And that would be a pity. You look so beautiful in it!"

Amelia knew that she had been a sad disappointment to Maggie, who no doubt envisioned an exciting career traveling from great house to great house when she took employment with a woman of quality. Instead, the poor girl's duties consisted primarily of easing plain, serviceable gowns over her mistress's head and arranging her hair, more often than not, in a simple knot at the nape of her neck instead of employing all the arts of adornment she had practiced so diligently when she first decided to better her status in life by becoming a lady's maid.

But no more.

Amelia was determined to present a smiling face to the world tonight.

He would have wanted it.

"My dear Amelia, you look dazzling!" Lady Madelyn exclaimed when Amelia came down the stairway of the British Embassy, where they were staying as guests of the government while Lady Madelyn completed her unofficial diplomatic mission.

Unlike many great beauties, Lady Madelyn was not in the least jealous of another woman's finery. Nor had she reason to be. She was dressed in a sea-green gauze gown with a peach satin wrap that made the most of her flawless gardenia-petal skin and gorgeous auburn hair. Emeralds glittered at her neck and earlobes.

"I cannot wait to introduce you to Count Briccetti," she added. "He is the most divine man, and a bachelor."

"That absurd fop," Lady Madelyn's husband scoffed good-naturedly. "My dear Miss Coomb, you will know the great man by the cloud of perfume that surrounds him and all the totty-headed women swooning in his wake."

Lady Madelyn batted her husband on the sleeve with her fan.

"Pay no attention to *him,* Amelia," she said airily. "He is insanely jealous merely because Count Briccetti paid a bit of attention to me before Robert and I were wed."

"He followed you to England from Italy and asked you to marry him," Robert reminded her. "I would hardly call that 'a bit of attention.' You would have accepted him, too, had I not barged into your house and put a stop to that nonsense."

"And I shall remember it always, dearest," Lady Madelyn said with a reminiscent smile on her lips.

Mr. Langtry closed his eyes and leaned expectantly toward his wife as she turned her face up to his.

Amelia politely looked away. Lady Madelyn and

Mr. Langtry were still so in love a year after their marriage that they tended to forget others were around.

Madelyn pushed gently against her husband's chest to remind him that they were not alone. He opened his eyes and gave her a fatuous smile, but she shook her head at him.

"I'm so sorry," she said, sounding conscience-stricken to Amelia. "It must be very difficult for you to witness such thoughtless displays while you are still grieving."

Amelia was startled.

"How did you know?" she asked. Indeed, she had taken great pains to act as if nothing out of the ordinary had occurred when she returned from praying for Father Dominic's soul.

"My dear, you know I never listen to gossip," Lady Madelyn began. She gave her husband a quelling look at his snort of amused skepticism. "But your cousin, Lady Blakely, is related by marriage to the Earl of Stoneham, and the earl's sister, Lady Letitia, is my godmother. I assure you that Lady Blakely spoke of your attachment to Lieutenant Lowell in the most discreet and sympathetic terms."

She was talking about Quentin.

Amelia's shameful secret, that she had fallen in love with a now-deceased Roman Catholic priest four years ago in Paris practically over poor Quentin's dead body, was safe.

"Your loyalty to Lieutenant Lowell's memory is evidence of a delicate sensibility," Lady Madelyn said, patting Amelia's hand. "But it is time to put your sorrow behind you."

"I do not deserve such praise," Amelia replied, flustered.

"You are so modest," Lady Madelyn said.

"Unlike someone I could mention," said her husband *sotto voce*.

His wife stared at him, and Mr. Langtry lifted both hands in feigned surrender.

"Perhaps you would be good enough to fetch our dominoes, dearest," Lady Madelyn said sweetly to her grinning spouse.

He gave her a mocking little bow and went off to obey.

Lady Madelyn fussed over Amelia's hair, moved one of the diamond combs from the back of her head slightly to the side, and twitched the gown's small puffed sleeves down so they displayed more of Amelia's shoulders.

"Thank you, Robert," she said as she took the red domino from her husband's hands when he returned from his errand. "I was going to wear this myself, but it would look better with your gown than the black, Amelia."

"I assure you I would not *dream* of taking your domino—"

"Nonsense. I can wear your black just as easily."

"But—"

"My dear, I insist!"

Madelyn draped the domino becomingly around Amelia's shoulders and handed her a small silver half-mask attached to a graceful wand. She thought that her friend looked absolutely lovely.

If any man could make Amelia forget her heartbreak, it was the perfectly *delicious* Count Andreas Briccetti. Madelyn couldn't wait for him to see her pretty protégée.

She ignored the tiny pang of envy this gave her.

In truth, Madelyn still had a soft spot in her heart for Andreas, although she would never admit as much to her husband. He had been so gracious when she declined his proposal in order to marry Robert, although Madelyn could sense his great disappointment. It had been a year and a half since Madelyn rejected the eligible count's suit, and still he was unmarried.

Madelyn was sincerely sorry to have broken his proud heart.

What could be more charming than to help these two attractive people find consolation in each other?

The mysterious depths of the Grand Canal were a bit too close for Amelia's peace of mind as she sat in the sleek gondola. All around her in the moonlit night, the water was full of the ghost-shadows of similar crafts. The laughter of their occupants echoed in the heavy air.

"Do not worry, darling," said Lady Madelyn, lounging at ease beside her. Mr. Langtry followed them in another gondola because the hired craft was too narrow to accommodate three persons comfortably. "Venetians have been traveling the canal in these gondolas for hundreds of years. This one will not tip over, I promise you."

"No, of course not," Amelia said with an uncertain smile. The gondolier stood up in back and used a pole to move the gondola through the water. Amelia had no idea what kept his weight from capsizing it.

"There is our destination," Lady Madelyn said excitedly. "Ca' Briccetti. Exquisite, is it not?"

"Exquisite," Amelia echoed dutifully as she peered into the ghostly mist beyond Lady Madelyn's pointing finger. The white marble palace glistened in the light of a dozen torches placed around the front. A party of gaily dressed men in various period costumes stood on the quay, laughing and jostling one another.

"There is Count Briccetti now," Lady Madelyn told

Amelia with a wave of her graceful hand toward a man standing on the quay. "My dear Andreas! How dashing you look!"

"Lady Madelyn!" the man exclaimed in a rich, melodious voice as he walked forward to meet their gondola. "How kind of you to come to my party now that you have broken my poor heart! Did you bring your husband with you? Will you permit me to throw him into the lagoon and make passionate love to you?"

Amelia had looked over her shoulder to smile at Mr. Langtry, whose craft had pulled up next to theirs, but the sound of that distinctive baritone made her whip her head around and stare with her mouth open. She rose to her feet so quickly that the gondola started to rock, but she ignored the gondolier's exclamation of warning as unimportant.

Her mind must be playing tricks on her, for the voice was Father Dominic's. The precise English words were flavored with the seductive Italian accent she remembered so well.

The man was turned slightly away from Amelia as he assisted Lady Madelyn from the gondola. He whispered something into that glamorous lady's ear that made her delightful tinkling laugh carry over the water.

When he turned politely to Amelia and offered his hand to assist her as well, the light from the torches fell on his handsome face.

Amelia gasped and clutched at her heart as if a dagger had suddenly pierced it. Then she screamed as she lost her balance and started to tumble backward.

The man darted forward and grabbed her shoulders to steady her.

For a moment they stared into each other's eyes.

It was he. Even had her eyes been struck blind, her flesh instantly would have recognized the touch of his hand. Her nostrils were filled with the exotic fragrance of his spicy cologne.

Father Dominic looked much the same as he had four years ago, only tonight he was in fancy dress for the masquerade ball. His ivory shirt was open at the throat to display the same jeweled crucifix he had worn in Paris. His snug breeches, dashing cavalier hat with jaunty feathers, and long, billowing cape were in royal blue.

"Look at that! They cannot take their eyes off each other," Lady Madelyn said in a self-congratulatory whisper to her husband. It carried quite clearly to Amelia's ears.

That broke the spell.

"Welcome to my home," the traitorous liar said softly as he took Amelia's gloved hand and assisted her from the gondola.

Amelia was so overcome by emotion that she clenched her teeth. She couldn't very well slap his face before Lady Madelyn and his other guests, so she gave a cry of frustration, seized his fancy hat, and threw it into the canal instead.

"Amelia!" cried Lady Madelyn, absolutely scandalized.

Incredibly, he laughed.

Then Amelia lost her head and pushed with both hands against his chest.

His eyes widened, and Amelia heard a collective gasp rise around her as he windmilled with his arms for a precarious moment over the dark waters of the canal. Then cheers and applause broke out when he succeeded in swinging his balance over the quay and safety. He took a bow to acknowledge the applause, but he kept one wary eye on Amelia.

"Beast!" she snarled just under her breath.

"I can explain—" he began.

"I doubt it," she snapped.

"On the dance floor," he said, ignoring her interruption. Then he grasped Amelia's hand and whisked her into the palace.

"Well, she certainly succeeded in capturing his attention," she heard Lady Madelyn say behind her.

"You are a scoundrel, sir," the Englishwoman said with a forced smile on her lips for the benefit of Count Briccetti's other guests.

At least she wasn't going to slap his face in the middle of the ballroom after all. It hadn't been difficult to read her first intention. His innocent English flower had yet to learn the useful art of dissembling.

"I can explain," he said again. His intentions in deceiving her had been pure. At least at first. But there was absolutely no excuse for having permitted the masquerade to go on for so long, and he knew it.

"I went from church to church all over the blessed city, looking for you."

"Did you?" he asked, absurdly touched that she would do such a thing.

She gave him a scornful look, and he made a small gesture of apology.

"I found a Father Dominic Soranzo—a *dead* Father Dominic Soranzo. I prayed by your—his—*grave!* I spent an hour on my *knees* in that church."

"Oh, my poor Miss Coomb," he said in dismay. "I am so very sorry."

She gave a little snarl of frustration.

"You have made a *fool* of me!"

"No, never that," he said gently as he took her hand, turned it over, and kissed her wrist where the tender flesh was bared for an inch between the tiny pearl buttons of her kid evening gloves.

She snatched back her hand as if he had burned her.

"That will be enough of *that,* sir! I have been most cruelly deceived!"

"I cannot say I am entirely sorry when it has brought you to my house," he said, and meant it. "You look magnificent. I have thought of you often these four years and prayed that you would find happiness."

"Never mind trying to turn me up sweet!" Several heads swiveled toward them in curiosity. She lowered her voice. "I have heard of men who take advantage of gullible females for their sport. What I do not understand is what you hoped to gain by it."

"Well, I could not say for sure, never having played such games," he said carefully, "but I *believe* the object is to gain certain favors from the lady that she otherwise might not be willing to bestow—"

She blushed scarlet.

"That will do," she said hastily. "But since you made no attempt—that is, since your behavior was of all things gentlemanly until—"

She looked away in confusion.

"Until you kissed me," he said softly.

"I was so ashamed," she admitted.

Even now his lips tingled in remembrance of that earnest kiss.

"As was I. May we agree to forget it?"

"Forget it?" She looked adorably confused.

"As if it never happened."

"Well, of course," she said, trying without success to look blasé. "It was nothing so very memorable, as I recall."

"Perhaps you recall the incident differently, then," he could not help saying. "It is not often that such very young ladies honor me in so charming a manner.

She blushed again.

Such an innocent.

A chuckle escaped his smiling lips. She was absolutely enchanting.

"How can you *laugh* about it?" she said, sounding hurt. "I thought you were *dead!*"

Andreas threw his hands up in exasperation.

"So you have said! It devastates me to disappoint you!"

"Don't be absurd!"

"Am I? You have a curious penchant for men who are cold and dead in their graves."

"What is *that* supposed to mean?" she demanded.

"Nothing. I apologize," he said at once. "I should not have said that."

"It is unfair and untrue! How could you say something so cruel to me?"

Her chin was quivering. He felt like a monster.

"You are right," he assured her. He remembered her genuine grief as she stood before the lieutenant's grave. He would never forget the guilt and confusion on her face when he kissed her. She thought she had tempted a chaste man to sin, poor girl. "You must forgive me, Miss Coomb. I am a little drunk."

True, he had imbibed freely of the imported champagne from his extensive cellars, but that wasn't what made him blurt out such an insensitive remark.

I am jealous, he realized.

Not of the dead lieutenant but of the priest for whose soul she had prayed an hour on her knees.

"I never meant to deceive you—" he began, but before he could finish his thought, the music ended and an imperative hand fell on his shoulder.

"Perhaps Miss Coomb will honor me with the next dance," said a voice that would not be denied.

Andreas rolled his eyes toward Lady Madelyn's tiresome husband, who apparently had appointed himself the guardian of Miss Coomb's virtue. Mr. Langtry had that stubborn look on his face that told Andreas he would happily engage to settle the matter with his fists if he did not unhand the young lady at once.

For a moment Andreas considered inviting the gentleman to step outside in a rash attempt to assert his manhood. It was devastating to his pride for the world to think him a shallow, frivolous coward who cared for nothing except fine clothes, rich food, strong drink, and accommodating women.

He told himself he could not permit his irrational desire to redeem his honor in Miss Coomb's eyes to expose his masquerade now. Not when he and his co-conspirators were so close to achieving their goal.

Besides, Mr. Langtry's wife was part of the key to success, and Andreas would hardly endear himself to the lady by bloodying the fellow's nose. For all her delicate appearance, Lady Madelyn's influence in British government circles was enormous. She could bring him the all-important support of England's might in his country's struggle for independence from the Austrians. Now that Lady Madelyn had come to Venice on some other pretext, he had the perfect opportunity to broach the matter of a possible alliance between the Venetians and the British to her without the Austrians suspecting his true intentions.

Having to endure the contempt in Miss Coomb's clear blue eyes was a small price to pay when weighed against freedom for his countrymen.

The House of Briccetti had a long, illustrious history of serving Venice. Andreas refused to be the first bearer of that proud name to fail his beloved Veneto when she needed him most.

"Of course, dear fellow," Andreas purred. "While you are dancing with Miss Coomb, I will engage to entertain your so-lovely wife."

He sauntered off with every appearance of nonchalance, but he could feel two pairs of eyes boring into his shoulder blades with deadly intent.

"It is not for me to criticize, Andreas," Lady Madelyn murmured as the count kissed her dainty fingers with practiced elegance, "but Robert is quite violently jealous of your attentions to me."

"I am aware of that," he said with a smile of indifference. "May I call on you tomorrow to discuss a very interesting proposition? Alone?"

She gave a flirtatious trill of laughter, but her eyes were shrewd.

"I hardly know how to answer such a bold request, my dear count," she cooed.

"In the affirmative," he said in an undervoice, although the smile never left his lips. "It is a matter of the utmost urgency."

"Then how can I refuse? You may call on me tomorrow at two o'clock. I shall find some errand upon which to send my husband and Miss Coomb. What do you think of my friend Miss Coomb, by the way? Quite enchanting, is she not?"

"I suppose I might find her so," he drawled, "if her charms were not so completely eclipsed by yours."

Lady Madelyn rapped him on the shoulder with her fan.

"Behave," she said, although she seemed more amused than annoyed. "Robert is casting quite murderous looks at the two of us."

"Let him believe my object is only to captivate his wife," he whispered. "It is the more harmless interpretation."

Lady Madelyn gave him a sharp look.

"I shall anticipate your visit tomorrow with great eagerness," she said with apparent pleasure for the benefit of any auditors. She gave him a languishing look and directed an airy little wiggle of her fingers toward a group of several highly placed Austrian government officials who broke off their discussion at once to smile and bow fervently in her direction.

What a woman, Andreas thought in admiration.

Just the same, he barely repressed the impulse to cross himself. There but for the grace of God, he thought as he encountered a glare from Lady Madelyn's hopelessly besotted husband, go I.

"Mr. Langtry," Amelia Coomb said to recall her dance partner to a sense of his surroundings. "My hand is quite numb, and I fear I will lose the use of it entirely if you do not relax your grip a little."

He was instantly contrite, although he continued to keep an eye on Count Andreas Briccetti. When the count escorted Lady Madelyn from the dance floor, blew her a kiss in parting and began to flirt outrageously with another lady, Mr. Langtry turned his full attention to Miss Coomb.

"My apologies for neglecting you, Miss Coomb," he said. "That useless fribble never fails to set my back up."

He gave her a smile with no mirth in it.

"Do not fall in love with him, I beg of you," he warned. "There is something ruthless about the fellow, for all his prancing and practiced compliments. Something I cannot quite like."

"Is he so bad, then?" Amelia asked. She scolded herself for the plaintive tone of her voice. She already knew Count Briccetti was a vile deceiver. She had never been so disillusioned in her life.

Mr. Langtry gave a snort of disgust.

"Look at him," he said with an inclination of his head toward the other end of the room, where the count was laughing uproariously at some remark made by an Austrian officer with a chest full of decorations, medals, and ribbons. The count threw an affectionate arm around the fellow's shoulders. "Every feeling revolts at the way he panders to the Austrians to court their favor."

"He seems so . . . otherwise," she said. She had been about to say honorable. Or heroic. But that was Father Dominic. The man he had only pretended to be.

"Yes, impressive fellow, isn't he? It was a bad moment when I thought Madelyn would have him."

The music ended.

"May I procure a cup of punch for you? Or some cakes?" he asked.

"No, nothing, I thank you."

"Do not look so put out, my dear Miss Coomb," Mr. Langtry said. "You are much too sensible to be taken in by the count's nonsense. A word to the wise, eh? I am confident the warning is unnecessary."

"Yes," she said, forcing herself to smile. "Quite unnecessary."

Count Briccetti looked across the room at that moment and caught Amelia's eye. He gave her a charming smile and a regal inclination of his handsome head.

She deliberately turned her back on him.

A word to the wise, indeed, she told her traitorous heart.

Six

"Your request is most intriguing, my dear Andreas," Lady Madelyn said as she passed the plate of ripe peaches and dainty cakes to her guest. "I can only speculate that my government would be interested in entertaining it, you understand. I have no official position with the diplomatic service and can hardly make a firm commitment on its behalf."

"I understand perfectly, Lady Madelyn," said the count, "but only someone naive in the ways of the world could underestimate the influence your informal opinions have on those who make policy for your government."

"Just so," she said with a gracious inclination of her head. Lady Madelyn knew her own worth and did not insult Andreas's intelligence with a show of false humility. It was one of the qualities he liked most about her. "I ask purely from idle curiosity, but what is it that you would offer my government in exchange for its assistance in winning your country's independence from Austria? Quite apart from the thanks of a grateful nation, that is?"

Andreas bent forward to look her straight in the eye, like any earnest negotiator.

"The greater part of my personal fortune in gold. A portion of the works of art that the Corsican and

the Austrians have not already extracted from Ca'
Briccetti and my villa on the mainland. The use of our
seaport as a military base and the services of our countrymen to fight at your side in the event that Britain
should once again find itself involved in a European
war. The use of my entire fleet of ships at your country's request in time of war as well. "

"Then, my dear count, I believe your country and
mine may be able to do business. I say this quite in-
formally, you comprehend."

"Of course."

For discretion's sake, they had conducted their conversation in Russian, ostensibly because Lady Madelyn wanted to practice her skill in that language—and
because lovers often employ a tongue different from
that of the servants for dalliance. In the unlikely event
that any of the servants actually understood Russian,
they kept their heads together and their voices low.

No one must know that they were involved in pre-
liminary negotiations for obtaining Great Britain's aid
in overthrowing the present government of Venice. Andreas could be executed as a traitor by the Austrians.
True, an influential British citizen such as Lady Madelyn could not be harmed for fear of perpetrating an
embarrassing international incident, but she could be
incarcerated, questioned, and expelled permanently
from the country. Thus, her status as an informal op-
erative in Great Britain's diplomatic service would be
seriously compromised.

Andreas was about to whisper an inquiry into Lady
Madelyn's ear about how soon she could broach the
matter with her government as he held a tantalizing
slice of ripe peach to her lips, but the lady's husband
chose that moment to barge in on them with Miss
Coomb and his two elder wards in tow.

"It is the little Melanie!" the count said with a

charming smile at Mr. Langtry's dark-haired, brown-eyed niece as he reached for her hand to enfold it in both of his. "What a beautiful young lady you have become in the time since I have last seen you. And Miss Coomb."

Amelia merely gave him a reserved inclination of her head, but Melanie seemed delighted to see him.

"Count Briccetti," she exclaimed. Her face lit up with pleasure. "If we had known you intended to call this afternoon, I am sure we would have stayed home. Mark and I were so disappointed that we couldn't attend your masquerade ball. It would have been such fun!" She directed a pretty pout at her uncle. "Uncle Robert says we are too young to attend such affairs, but I thank you for remembering us."

"It was my very great pleasure, pretty one," the count said gallantly. "Perhaps another time."

"Not bloody likely," Mr. Langtry said pleasantly. He stepped in front of his niece as if to defend the girl from the count's salacious advances. Melanie peeked around him to give Andreas a humorous look of commiseration.

"I say," Mark commented as he reached forward to shake hands with the count. "Are those custard cakes?" He started to take one, but a glare from his uncle caused him to step back and send an interrogative look toward his sister. She shrugged.

The count sprawled arrogantly on the sofa and lifted his glass of lemonade as if in a toast. "Mr. Langtry. What an unexpected pleasure."

"*Is* it?" that gentleman asked with one arched eyebrow.

"Darling," said Lady Madelyn with a bright artificial smile at her spouse. Andreas speculated it would take all her arts of persuasion to calm the fellow down when he left. He hoped she would not have too bad a time of it. "I told Count Briccetti that I expected you to be occupied all afternoon sight-seeing with Miss Coomb and the children."

"So sorry to disappoint you," he said with a snort of disdain in Andreas's direction. As always, Andreas marveled at Lady Madelyn's sincere attachment to this gauche Englishman. Especially since she could have had *him*.

"Don't be ridiculous, dearest," Lady Madelyn said to her husband with a gay, tinkling laugh. "Sit down and join us for some lemonade and cakes." She made a graceful gesture with her hands toward the chairs opposite the sofa. "Amelia. Mark. Melanie. Please."

"Thank you, no," Miss Coomb said, staring at Andreas as if he were the lowest form of life on earth. "I have letters to write."

"I trust you are finding my country hospitable, Miss Coomb," the count said. "I enjoyed our dance. You will honor me again some evening, I hope."

She did not dignify this comment with a reply.

"Mark and I have letters to write too," Melanie said with a significant look at her brother. Mark had started to seat himself on the sofa on the other side of Lady Madelyn, but he stopped to raise an eyebrow at Melanie. She nodded toward Mr. Langtry. A wary glance at his uncle had Mark straightening and making his excuses as he followed his sister from the room.

Andreas suppressed a smile at Mr. Langtry's tight-lipped expression. The finest actor in the world could not have conveyed jealousy so convincingly. Andreas was certain at this point that Lady Madelyn had given her husband no hint that his intimate tête-à-tête with her was anything but personal, for which he was exceedingly grateful.

When the embassy servants gossiped to their counterparts in other houses—as Andreas had no doubt they would—their tales would be of marital infidelity and jealous husbands instead of treason and insurrection.

"You have overstayed your welcome, Count Briccetti," Mr. Langtry said in a voice that brooked no argument. "Take yourself off, if you please, or I shall be happy to escort you outside."

He clenched and unclenched his fists suggestively.

"Robert!" exclaimed Lady Madelyn at this rudeness.

Miss Coomb's eyes widened. Could it be she was reluctant to see Mr. Langtry beat him to a bloody pulp?

Andreas did not flatter himself that this was so.

"Certainly, my dear fellow. Certainly," the count drawled, forcing himself to cringe a little to support his persona of cowardly fop. He took Lady Madelyn's hand and pressed a fervent kiss on the back of it. Then he stood and made her a courtly bow. "Until we meet again, and I hope it will be soon."

"Do not make me ask you to name your friends, sir," the jealous husband said. He stepped between the count and his wife.

Miss Coomb gasped.

"Robert, for pity's sake," Lady Madelyn protested.

"I will be happy to name my friends, if it pleases you, my dear Mr. Langtry," Andreas said audaciously. "I name Lady Madelyn and Miss Coomb."

Langtry sighed and started to remove his coat.

"I see you are determined to force the issue," he said. "Very well. Outside. We do not want to distress the ladies with the sight of *your* blood."

Lady Madelyn took her husband's arm and snuggled under it.

"Darling," she said. "Do not be absurd. Count Briccetti is completely harmless."

"This is true," Andreas said with an alacrity he could tell did him no credit in Miss Coomb's eyes. "I admire your lady from afar, as always."

Mr. Langtry allowed himself to be mollified by his wife's attentions.

"I shall go now," Andreas said. He crooked his arm in Miss Coomb's direction. "Will you lend me your support to the door, my dear young lady? I feel faint all of a sudden."

He expected her to flounce off in disgust, but she surprised him by accepting the arm.

"You should be ashamed of yourself for trying to make trouble between Lady Madelyn and her husband," she scolded as they walked toward the front hall.

"Carissima," he said reproachfully.

"Do *not* call me that," she said from between clenched teeth. "I am wise to your tricks, remember?"

He cupped her cheek in his hand.

"You are still angry about Paris," he said softly. She blushed and looked away. "What must I do to earn your forgiveness?" He turned her face back to his and bent to kiss her. She smelled like cherry blossoms and sunshine.

"You are utterly disgusting!" she said as she pushed against his chest to extricate herself from his loose embrace.

He couldn't agree more.

"You can see yourself out," she snapped. She turned her back on him and fairly ran back into the main part of the house.

Andreas suffered a pang of regret.

He wanted nothing more than to reassure her that his intentions in Paris had been all that was honorable and respectful.

Instead, as he intended, she thought he was a heartless rake.

So be it.

He could not afford to be distracted by her pretty face while he was engaged in a mission so fraught with danger.

By giving her a disgust of him, Andreas had effectively removed her from sharing that danger. It was a greater sacrifice than she would ever know.

Robert Langtry was, by all accounts, judged to be a bluff, good-natured, hopelessly besotted country squire who was wrapped quite securely around his imperious wife's little finger.

He was not, however, a fool.

Madelyn bit her lip and looked down at her clasped hands, the very picture of a chastened wife, as her husband loomed over her.

He had to admit she did it well.

"Suppose you tell me what you are up to, my dear. And please do not insult my intelligence by pretending you are having an affair with Count Briccetti."

She arched one intelligent eyebrow at him.

"And why not? He is universally accounted to be excessively attractive."

"Yes, and rich. And sophisticated. I have no doubt most ladies would give just about anything you care to name to be the object of his attentions. But I do not believe *you* are of their number."

"You believed," she said. "I saw the look on your face when you found him here."

"Maybe at first," he acknowledged. "Unfortunately, I came to my senses before I planted my fist in his pretty face."

"Quite awfully sure of yourself, are you not?" Her head was thrown back in challenge.

"Completely. If you were having an affair with another man, you would not be standing there wringing your hands like a penitent little wife waiting to be punished. I know you too well. You would protest your innocence in the most effective way possible—by manipulating me into your bed so you could put my unworthy suspicions at rest."

"True," she said, smiling. She reached up to put her graceful hands on each side of his face. She rose on tiptoe so her lips were an inch away from his. "I suppose it is too late for that now."

"Not at all," he said.

He kissed her, then put an arm around her shoulders to guide her upstairs to her boudoir. She snuggled close to his side and rested her head on his shoulder.

"Darling?" he murmured.

"Yes?"

"If you cannot tell me what you are doing, you will at least promise me to be careful, will you not?"

"I do not know what you mean," she said, and kissed him again.

"For if something happened to you," he said solemnly as he pulled the blue ribbon from her hair and allowed the rich mass of loose red curls to cascade over her slim shoulders, "I would not want to live."

Madelyn put her arms around his waist and held him close. He kissed the top of her head and breathed in the fragrance of her perfumed hair.

Supported by his arms, she arched her back and looked up into his eyes.

"I will be careful, my love," she promised, and led him into the darkened room.

Seven

Amelia knew the man she sought was not here. He had never been here. In truth, he had never existed.

Yet as she knelt once again in the cool half-darkness of the little church redolent of beeswax and incense, she felt at peace, and she needed peace very badly.

Indeed, the man she once had loved so sincerely was more lost to her now than when she had thought him dead.

"Still mourning dead men, Miss Coomb?" a voice echoed behind her in eerily hollow tones.

For a moment Amelia imagined it was *his* voice. And when she looked up, it appeared to be *his* body silhouetted against the light coming in through the stained glass.

Then he stepped closer, and she could see him clearly.

It was merely the odious Count Briccetti after all.

"Why not? In many ways dead men are infinitely more satisfactory than the living," she replied, annoyed that the irritating man had come to disturb her here.

Only a blind woman would have mistaken him for a priest today. He was dressed in the first stare of fashion—bottle-green coat, buff pantaloons, tall, supple boots. The well-to-do gentleman at leisure.

He sauntered forward to loom over her.

"Obviously, my dear, you do not know the right men."

She gave him a withering look.

"I did once. And he was a sham."

He took her hands and gently pulled her to her feet.

"Not quite. Come."

Puzzled, she accompanied him to the grave the priest had shown her that first day in Venice.

When they reached it, the count inclined his head toward the headstone in the garden. Amelia had been distraught that first day upon learning Father Dominic Soranzo was dead, so she had missed the obvious.

The stone was small, but it was not a simple priest's memorial. The stone was of pure white marble. The lettering, the stylized cross, and flowing decorations at the corners had been chiseled by an artist of the first magnitude.

Now she did what did not occur to her then.

She bent down and moved some of the blossoms slightly so she could read the lettering that had been hidden by them.

Father Dominic Soranzo
Devoted Servant of Our Lord
and Loyal Son of Venice
1760–1818

May he rest in peace

Amelia rose and peered into the count's shadowed face. There was real sorrow in it.

"Who was he?" she asked.

"A simple priest."

"That is *what* he was. *Who* was he? To you, I mean."

She thought for a moment he would not answer.

"My tutor. My mentor. And my friend. I will miss him every day for the rest of my life." He looked into her eyes. "I told him about you."

"About *me?*" Amelia had not expected this.

"In Paris. One of the reasons I went to Paris was to visit him at a convent there. I had arranged for the good sisters to take him in after he became a hunted man in Venice."

"He was a criminal?" she asked with a frown.

"A patriot," he said. "A saint."

"A saint," she repeated, thinking of the kind priest who helped her survive the worst days of her life.

"I took his name when you thought I was a priest. Perhaps I acted on a lifelong desire to be like him." He looked down again at the marble monument.

"I am sorry," she said, sensing his heartfelt loss.

"You mourn the man you knew in Paris, and I regret that. But I tell you he was a pale shadow of the real Father Dominic Soranzo. He spoke out against the oppressors of Venice while I, his student, drank and gambled with them, and gave them bribes to keep them from interfering with my business interests while my countrymen suffered under their yoke. I wish you could have met him."

"Why do you tell me this?"

"I would not be responsible for stealing away your faith in good men," he said with a rueful smile. "I am not the man you thought, but this does not mean such men do not exist."

"Perhaps you were the wiser man," Amelia said bitterly. "You are alive, as your Father Dominic is not. As Quentin is not."

He smiled at her and raised her hand to his lips. In another chameleon change of personality, he was, once again, the charming man she met at the ball.

"True," he said. "It does not do to involve oneself in political issues. Better to accept what cannot be changed and enjoy one's life."

"Better to use one's life for the betterment of man," she said reprovingly.

"Yes! And what better man than I? Come. We have spent enough time among dead men, you and I. Now that we no longer have a vow of celibacy between us . . ."

Incredibly, he bent as if he would kiss her. For a moment her nostrils were full of the spicy scent she remembered so well, and she swayed toward him.

Then she drew back and averted her eyes.

"Pity," he said with a theatrical sigh as he placed a fleeting kiss on her cheek. "Come. I will take you back to the city in my gondola. All the ladies like to ride with me in my gondola. It is pretty and superficial—like me."

His did it well, but his attitude of joviality was false.

"What did you tell him? About me, I mean."

"Father Dominic? That you were innocent and troubled and I took his name because I suspected if you knew the truth of my identity you would not let me watch over you." His smile had a wry twist to it. "I think he was amused. And oddly pleased. He took it as a sign that I was a better man than he had thought."

"Innocent and troubled," she repeated. "How pathetic I must have seemed to you."

"Courageous. And trusting," he corrected her. "Do not underestimate yourself, *carissima*," he said. "You are stronger than you think. More suspicious. More selfish. Like me."

"Selfish! Like *you!* I am *nothing* like you!" Amelia was filled with indignation. "How can you say that?"

"Is it not selfish to condemn those less fortunate than yourself to oppression by their enemies rather than endanger oneself? Oh, do not misunderstand. I can only admire such pragmatism."

"You know nothing about me," she said angrily. "I have dedicated my *life* to the less fortunate!"

"You have brought them baskets of bread and soup," he said. "You have advised them to be patient and grateful for what they have. I merely suggest that a population of patient and grateful peasants is a useful thing for their betters."

"How could I have thought you were a saint?"

"How indeed? Come with me, my sweet, and be the envy of all your friends. It is too fine a day to be drooping over graves."

"I have asked the gondolier who brought me here to wait. I will return to the city with him."

"That will prove difficult, I fear," he said, "for I have dismissed him."

She huffed with indignation and was about to ring a peal over his head for such high-handedness, but before she could do so, the chiseled monument caught her eye.

"What is he doing here?" she asked, indicating the grave.

"Rotting, what else?" he said with a shrug. "It is what all dead men do."

"He was a political outcast expelled from his country by the Austrian authorities for fostering insurrection," she said thoughtfully. "How does he come to be buried here, unless someone with powerful connections intervened on his behalf?"

"I had him brought here when his health failed and he wished to die in the country he loved," the count said. "I entreated on his behalf with my very good friends, the Austrians, and rewarded them for their mercy with a bribe. His last days were peaceful ones, cultivating this garden and saying Mass in the church when his health permitted it. He still persisted in working among the poor, though, and that killed him in the end. His dream had failed, and it was buried with him."

"You were a good friend to him."

"This is true," he agreed. "After all, it did not require a very *large* bribe to convince the Austrians to permit him to return."

"I think you are not so bad as you pretend to be," she said.

He gave a snort of laughter, but there was little mirth in it.

"And before I was not so good as I pretended to be," he said. "This is not sensible, your habit of expecting men to be saints. It will only lead to disappointment. I have had enough of this serious conversation. You will come with me in my gondola, yes?"

A woman of stronger convictions would have *swum* back to the city rather than accept his escort.

The uncomfortable truth was that—much as she deplored his frivolity and selfishness—she found the count's conversation stimulating. He, at least, did not expect her to be the docile, submissive young lady. He knew more about her secret soul than anyone alive, even if that knowledge was gained under false pretenses.

Amelia gave a nod of assent and permitted the count to lead her away from the lovingly tended grave and onto the quay where his gondola lay at anchor. The count's boast had not been an idle one. The gondola was black, like all the others she had seen in Venice, but it had ornately carved gold-leaf trim and red velvet cushions. On the sleek, gracefully curved front was a small gilded carving, a sort of figurehead, in the form of what appeared to be some classical god, such as

Apollo or Adonis. She looked from it to the count and noted the resemblance.

The vain creature must have modeled for it himself.

"It is accounted to be the artist's finest work," he said, demonstrating that uncanny ability to read her mind. "How could he not be inspired by such a perfect form?"

She absolutely had to laugh. It was difficult not to be amused by his conceit.

The gondolier touched the brim of his hat respectfully to Amelia and would have assisted her into the gondola, but the count waved him away with one languid hand as if the man had been a pesky fly.

He took Amelia's right hand in his and placed his other hand at the small of her back. She could feel the warmth of his skin through her thin muslin gown.

He sprawled at her side after he had seated her and casually removed his green coat. He wore no waistcoat under it, and the wind molded the fine ivory linen of his flowing shirt to his powerful shoulders and broad chest.

"See here! What are you doing?" she cried in alarm at both his state of undress and the way his movements caused the gondola to rock.

"Do not be frightened, my dear," he said, grinning at her discomfiture. "This is all I will remove—for now."

"So I should hope!"

"The sun is hot. Do not hesitate to remove any of your own clothing on my account," he said magnanimously.

"How very kind," she said sarcastically. "But I think not."

Now that he had removed his coat, Amelia could see he was wearing that jeweled crucifix against his chest, the one that had misled her into thinking he was a priest four years ago.

"Why do you wear that?" she asked.

"The shirt? I can remove it if you wish." She frowned at his show of eagerness. Apparently tiring of the game, he removed the crucifix and handed it to her. It was even heavier than it looked.

"It was a gift from the Doge of Venice to one of my ancestors. The heads of our house have worn it since."

"And what did your ancestor do to deserve it?" she asked as she handed it back to him.

The indulgent smile had a note of sadness in it as he replaced the chain around his neck.

"He defeated Venice's enemies on the sea. He died a hero two years later in another battle." He gave a mock salute. "A lesson to us all that heroic gestures are likely to be fatal."

She made no comment because her attention was arrested by a man waving his arms from some small craft ahead.

"Your pardon, Miss Coomb," the count said with excruciating politeness. "Am I boring you?"

"Those people seem to be in some trouble."

Andreas squinted and peered across the sunlit waters in the direction she indicated.

"For God's love, signore!" a man shouted in Italian from the stalled craft. "The boat, she has sprung a leak!"

The count shrugged and smiled at Amelia. "Now. Where were we, my dear? That fellow has made me lose the thread of our conversation. I apologize."

"Please, Excellency! I do not swim! And my wife, she does not swim either!" the man shouted, even though Amelia knew he could not have heard the count's comment. The wife's bowed head was veiled in a dark shawl.

"He may drown, and his poor wife with him!" Amelia cried.

"You do not know these simple folk, Miss Coomb. They exaggerate everything. It is not deep here. I do not think," Andreas said.

"Signore?" the count's gondolier said. He was looking at his employer with surprise and consternation.

The count burst into laughter.

"Pull in close on the left, Bassanio, so I can reach the woman," he said to the gondolier.

He had meant to rescue the couple all along. Amelia didn't know whether she wanted to kiss him or slap him hard enough to make his ears ring!

When they were almost abreast of the disabled craft, the man leaned over his wife, who appeared to be bailing the water from the boat with a small container of some kind. The count stood up and crossed in front of Amelia with one arm extended.

"Take my hand, signora," the count said soothingly in Italian to the woman, who crouched away from him as if she were afraid. She pulled the shawl over her eyes. "I will not let you fall."

While the count's attention was on the woman, her companion suddenly stood up and a shot rang out. Amelia heard a splash behind her.

"Andreas!" she cried out as the count pushed her to the floor and covered her body with his. Crushed under his weight, she could feel his heart pounding against her face. "Andreas! Count Briccetti! Are you hit?"

"No," he said, rising slightly and bracing himself on his elbows on either side of her. "Are you all right?" His mouth was inches from hers.

"Yes. Of course," she said. Relief made her testy. "No one was shooting at *me!*"

"Good girl," he said, and gave her a fleeting kiss on the lips. "Stay here and keep your head down. Do not make a sound. Bassanio was hit."

The splash must have been the gondolier falling into the water. Now the count, to her amazement, jumped in after him.

Amelia could not lie there, cowering like a frightened animal. Cautiously, she rose on one elbow and peered out of the gondola to see the gunman rowing his boat toward shore with all haste.

"The villain," she cried out.

She screamed when a sleek head popped out of the water in front of her.

"I told you . . . to stay down," Andreas gasped, but there was no real anger in it. He had Bassanio in a hold across his shoulders, and his other hand gripped the side of the gondola, which caused it to dip alarmingly. The gondolier was conscious and sputtering. "Can you hold him . . . by the shirt?"

"Yes," she said, and reached to grasp the wet fabric. When she did, the gondola rocked, but she held on tightly to keep the man's head out of the water.

"Good," Andreas said as he levered himself out of the water and into the gondola. He looked down ruefully at his sodden clothes and ruined boots. "My valet is going to have the vapors when he sees this."

Amelia tore her eyes away from him after a shocked instant. He might as well have been naked.

"I'll take him now," he said, oblivious to her embarrassment. With an impressive show of strength, he reached into the water, grabbed the gondolier, and hauled him into the boat.

Amelia could not suppress a screech of alarm at the way the craft rocked when he did so.

"Steady, Miss Coomb," the count said absently as he ripped the gondolier's sodden shirt off at the neckline to lay the wound bare. "The bullet seems to have lodged in his shoulder."

The gondolier gave a sharp intake of breath.

"The poor man," Amelia said.

"Poor man? Not so, my dear. You are a lucky man, Bassanio, that it did not find your heart. Of course, the bullet will have to be dug out."

"I am . . . not . . . going to die?" the man asked in relief between gasps of pain.

"No, Bassanio. You have nothing to fear." He turned to Amelia. "This wound must be stanched before he loses any more blood. I would gladly sacrifice my shirt if it were not soaking wet, but I'm afraid I must beg your indulgence, dear lady. Have you a clean item of apparel you could spare? Preferably of white linen?"

"Of course," she said, reaching into her abandoned reticule and withdrawing a handkerchief.

"Pity. I was hoping for a length of petticoat," he said with a wicked smile as he accepted it. He looked at it a moment in surprise and smirked. "Interesting."

Amelia could feel herself blush.

It was one of his from four years ago. She had treasured it all this time as a sort of talisman. And now he knew.

"*Signore,*" whispered Bassanio. He tried to sit up.

"No, Bassanio," the count said, putting a strong hand on his good shoulder to prevent him. "You must lie still."

"My wife! My children!" Bassanio burst out. "What is to become of them?"

"Do not worry, my friend. I will take care of them until you can work again. Could I do otherwise when you took the bullet meant for me?"

Amelia rocked back on her heels.

Someone had tried to kill him. In the excitement, she almost had forgotten that.

"Here, man," Andreas said in reproof when Bassanio seized his hand and covered it with kisses of gratitude. "No need for *that*."

"Count Briccetti!" called a voice from outside the gondola. Amelia looked across it to see Sir Gregory Banbridge, a senior British Embassy official, leaning over the side of another gondola to peer at them. In the gondola with him was Lady Madelyn. "Are you hurt?"

"No!" the count shouted back. "But my gondolier has been shot."

Sir Gregory frowned. He was a handsome, impeccably groomed man whose excellent tailoring could not completely disguise the damage that fine foods and vintage wines had done to a once-admirable figure.

"Amelia!" Lady Madelyn exclaimed with a frown. "What is the meaning of this?"

"I shall explain later," Amelia replied, frowning right back at her. Lady Madelyn was clearly appalled to find another woman with the count. And she had such a nice husband too.

"Do you need assistance?" Sir Gregory asked, although his tone was clearly reluctant.

"No," the count replied. "I will manage to get us to shore." He looked at Amelia. "Can you sit here, Miss Coomb, and stanch the wound?"

"Of course," she said as she slipped in beside the wounded man.

"You do not grow dizzy at the sight of blood, I hope?" he asked. Amelia shook her head. "That's a good girl. Hold the handkerchief like this and press hard." He took her hand and pressed it against the bloodied handkerchief to demonstrate.

"Very well, then," Sir Gregory said, signaling his gondolier to go on.

"We will go on ahead to your house and prepare your servants," Lady Madelyn said. "We will send one of them for a doctor." As the gondola pulled away, she looked back at them with concern in her eyes. The count had moved from her side to take the fallen gondolier's place at the back of the boat.

"She should be ashamed of herself!" Amelia said.

"Lady Madelyn?" Andreas asked. He had taken up the gondolier's pole and was moving the gondola along the canal with reasonable competence. "Why should she?"

Amelia started. She had not realized she spoke aloud. But since he asked, she had no hesitation in telling him.

"First, for flirting with you and making her husband jealous. And now she is rather too friendly with Sir Gregory if she is alone with him in a gondola. She seemed such a kind lady, always giving generously to the poor and working for the benefit of orphans."

"And so she is. Sir Gregory is married?"

"Well, no. He is a widower, but *she* is married."

"Lady Madelyn is in love with her husband. Never doubt it. But she is not dead. Of course she will look." He grinned. His strong teeth were blindingly white. "As you are looking now."

Amelia blushed and looked away. His wet clothes were really quite indecent, and she was annoyed that he caught her staring.

"Do not be embarrassed," he said kindly. "I am quite accustomed to the admiration of ladies."

Bassanio gave a surprised grunt.

"Oh, I am so sorry!" Amelia cried. She obviously was pressing down too hard on the wound.

"Bassanio! You are all right, yes?" the count called out cheerfully in Italian.

"Yes, signore," the gondolier said. "You will not forget about my wife and children, eh?"

"I will not, my friend," the count promised. Amelia's eyes misted at the note of kindness in his voice. He reminded her suddenly of the compassionate priest she had thought she knew so well.

They drew up to the quay in front of the Ca' Briccetti, and liveried servants ran forward to transfer Bassanio from the gondola to the shore. A concerned Lady Madelyn and Sir Gregory were with them.

"Are you quite all right, my dear Andreas?" Lady Madelyn said when Amelia and the count were on the quay. She looked worried. "You look pale."

"Now that the excitement is over, I feel quite . . . overcome," he said. He staggered, and Lady Madelyn and Sir Gregory moved forward quickly to grasp him by either arm and hold him upright. "The bullet was meant for me, you know," he said in a shaking voice.

"Yes, Andreas," Lady Madelyn said soothingly. "But you are safe now. Come into the house. You shall tell Sir Gregory and me all about it over a cup of hot tea. I have already ordered your housekeeper to bring it to the green salon. But first you must change out of those wet clothes. Your valet is waiting for you in your suite."

"Carissima, you are an angel," he murmured.

Amelia thought that they had forgotten all about her, but the count looked over his shoulder as Lady Madelyn and Sir Gregory supported his tottering steps to the palace.

"Come along, Miss Coomb. You must have a cup

of tea as well." He smiled boyishly at her. "You may tell Lady Madelyn how brave I was."

Amelia rolled her eyes and followed.

Eight

Andreas was still pale just after dusk when he entered the long-abandoned warehouse—but it was with anger rather than fear.

Ten men came out of the darkness; one carried a lighted lantern. Like Andreas, they were dressed in nondescript black. These were freedom fighters made up of former members of the *arsenalòtte,* a group of patriotic men who once worked in the republic's shipyards and armament works, and their sons. It was they who would provide the muscle for the coming revolt.

Indeed, the count believed, if the last doge had rallied the formidable men of the *arsenalòtte* to Venice's defense instead of abdicating without a fight to Napoleon in 1797, Venice might still be a republic instead of a mere section of the Austrian empire known as the Lombard-Veneto Kingdom. If Andreas had been seventeen instead of seven at the time, he gladly would have fought at their side.

Instead, he was forced to wage this clandestine war and discipline the fools among his co-conspirators who would sabotage their efforts from within.

Andreas looked from one dimly lighted figure to the other, made his choice, and stepped right up to hit the man hard in the face. Niccolò Soranzo staggered back with a grunt and rubbed his jaw. He alone among

Andreas's co-conspirators was descended from a family that had enjoyed aristocratic status in the days of the republic. He was, in fact, Father Dominic's nephew, and, though he shared the same blood, evidenced none of that good man's virtue and wisdom.

The others gave a collective gasp, but no one interfered.

"Did you think I would not see through your disguise, you *imbecile!*" the count demanded. "How *dare* you shoot my gondolier? I hope you can trust your woman to keep her mouth shut."

Niccolò gave a harsh laugh. He rubbed his jaw again.

"She knows I will stop her mouth up permanently if she does not. Those pampered hands of yours are not quite as soft as they look, *Count* Briccetti," he observed. The Austrian government had conferred this title upon Andreas in recognition of his generosity to Venice's oppressors, so Andreas knew very well that Niccolò invoked it now not in respect but in scorn. True sons of the Venetian aristocracy disdained such titles, but Andreas used it with outward pride as further camouflage for his true loyalties.

Such pragmatism was lost on Niccolò. Or so he pretended.

"The bastard is an Austrian spy," he spat out.

"Of course he is, you idiot! Do you think I did not know it?

Niccolò's eyes narrowed.

"Then you should thank me for shooting him."

"I should hit you again!" the count declared. Niccolò flinched. "Bassanio thought you were trying to shoot *me,* and he deliberately placed himself within the range of your bullet instead of trying to escape it. What does that tell you?"

"That he is stupid?"

"That he is willing to risk his life to save me," Andreas said in a voice dripping with contempt. "He has a wife and six children, and he is paid well by me for driving my gondola and equally well by the Austrians for spying on me. This ends if I die. I am safer with Bassanio guarding my back than I was in my own mother's womb. And now *you* have shot him!"

"It was past time to send the Austrians a show of strength," the culprit declared in ringing tones.

Andreas could sense the surge of approval that Niccolò's words inspired in some of the other conspirators, and he took immediate steps to quash it. Andreas, too, would derive immense satisfaction in fighting this battle like a man with his fists instead of like a coward with clandestine meetings and honeyed words dropped in the right foreign ears, but that was a luxury none of them could afford.

There were times when he actually envied Niccolò, even though his stupidity was likely to get him—or perhaps all of them—killed.

"My congratulations," Andreas said with a mocking smile. "You have now eliminated their spy—the spy who reports to them how idle and frivolous I am and thus allays any suspicion that I am a threat to their stranglehold over Venice—so now I must be on guard against the replacement they will inevitably put in my household. Meanwhile, I am pledged to support the man's wife and children until he can return to my service."

"Why should you care about his wife and children?" the man demanded. "He was spying on you."

"Because Count Andreas Briccetti is known as a soft-hearted fool who is overly indulgent with his women and his servants."

In an impressive demonstration of physical strength, the count snatched the man by his collar and held him up by one hand so his feet left the ground. Niccolò started to wheeze for breath as his windpipe was squeezed by his own weight.

After a moment, the count gave him a shove and he crumpled into a sitting position, rubbing his throat and cursing under his breath.

Andreas knew Niccolò would not soon forgive this insult to his manly pride. Since Father Dominic Soranzo's death, he had been tireless in his attempts to take over leadership of their band of conspirators. As the priest's nephew, he felt he had a right to lead them, but the count was not the only one who feared the violence and bitterness that seethed in the hot-headed Niccolò's heroic heart would lead them to exposure and death.

Andreas had to assert his authority over this man immediately in front of the others if he was to command their respect and obedience in the future.

"Remember, my friend, who is your leader," the count said in a low, threatening voice. "From now on, you make no movement without my permission."

"And you will do what? Sully your lily-white hands with the blood of a stinking peasant?" It pleased Niccolò to style himself so, even though his patrician heritage was almost as venerable as the count's. He apparently thought it gave him a certain peculiar legitimacy among the revolutionaries. He lived among them and cheerfully fought beside them in the brawls they incited in the wine shops. Indeed, he had little choice. His father, like most of the patricians in Venice, had been reduced to poverty during Napoleon's tenure as overlord of the city.

"If need be," the count told him. "These are dangerous times for all of us. Do not be misled by my reputation as a soft man. Act without my order again, and I will not hesitate to eliminate you. Get up! Get out! We are done here."

He deliberately turned his back to show the others he did not fear retribution from this dangerous young whelp, but his shoulder blades were prickling as he walked back to the place where he had docked his plain gondola—the one he rarely used in daylight—and poled it home himself.

Andreas had expected something of this sort from Niccolò. He had been a thorn in his side from the beginning, but Father Dominic—because of their family relationship and because the priest was a bit of a firebrand himself—had been able to control him easily.

The matter was settled for now, but it boded ill for the future.

Worst of all, the residents of the British Embassy were aware of the assassination attempt just when Andreas had been at great pains to convince the British that he was the undisputed leader of the conspiracy to overthrow the Austrians.

Lady Madelyn and, he was led to believe, Sir Gregory were sympathetic to Venice's cause. Use of a seaport on the Adriatic Sea in addition to the generous glorified bribes Andreas had offered the British from his own purse were strong incentives for them to support the rebellion.

But they would not hesitate to deny their support to a movement that might fail and compromise the British Empire's prestige as a world power. Nothing was more conducive to the failure of an uprising than dissension among the ranks of the conspirators.

Andreas quickly made his way back to the city, where he was committed to make an appearance at Lady Madelyn's soiree. It was of vital importance that he show himself to be intact but suitably intimidated by the supposed assassination attempt against him. The Austrians must be convinced that Andreas had no idea that Bassanio was their spy. And they must never suspect that Bassanio was the true target of the gunman.

"Are you quite recovered from your dreadful shock?" Lady Madelyn asked Andreas with concern in her eyes when he appeared at the British Embassy.

"Here, old fellow," Mr. Langtry said with an insincere smile. "Have a glass of wine."

Andreas allowed his hand to shake slightly as he accepted the crystal wineglass and meekly allowed Lady Madelyn to lead him to a white brocade sofa.

"I quite despaired of seeing you here tonight," Lady Madelyn said, but her eyes were alert. She was an old friend, and he knew he occupied a place in her heart as the man she almost married, but her primary loyalty was to her country, and she would not hesitate to withdraw her recommendation that Britain support the rebellion if she suspected that Andreas could not control his compatriots.

"Shall I fetch a vinaigrette?" Robert Langtry asked. Andreas was not fooled by his solicitous tone. "Madelyn, of course, never carries one. But surely some other lady would be willing to come to your aid."

Mr. Langtry smirked when several ladies eagerly stepped forward to press their vinaigrettes upon Andreas. Bless them, they used the opportunity to seat themselves around him and prevent Lady Madelyn from asking any awkward questions.

"Thank you, ladies, thank you," Andreas said, summoning a flutter to his voice. "But I have one of my own." Mr. Langtry gave a snort of contempt when Andreas withdrew a crystal vinaigrette from his breast pocket. "Of course, I had the courage of a lion. But once the danger was past, I must confess I took to my bed at once."

"A jealous husband no doubt," Mr. Langtry said quite cheerfully.

Andreas could have kissed him—this was the very impression he wished to leave with both the British and the Austrians. Let them believe that the assassination attempt was the result of Andreas's dalliance with some female. It was the interpretation that would do the least harm to his cause.

"I fear this is so," Andreas said in mock regret as he took a sustaining sip of the wine.

"Count Briccetti!" Sir Gregory said with bluff good humor. He could not quite suppress a sneer at the pathetic picture Andreas presented, languishing on the sofa with a vinaigrette clutched in one hand and a glass of champagne in the other as pretty ladies sat all around vying with one another to console him. "So pleased you are up to the ordeal of joining us after your unpleasant experience."

"I certainly would not allow such a trifling matter to discourage me from attending a party at the British Embassy."

"I am relieved to hear it," that gentleman said dryly before he moved on to greet other guests.

"I trust Miss Coomb has recovered from the ordeal as well?" Andreas inquired of Madelyn. He would have called at the embassy earlier to express his concern for her if he had not been obliged to languish on his bed for several hours, ostentatiously clutching a vinaigrette for the benefit of his house servants. He had no way of knowing if Bassanio had been the only Austrian spy in his employ. "I do not see her among your guests."

"She will be down directly," Madelyn replied. "Her mother arrived today—such a delightful surprise." Andreas nearly choked on his wine. Lady Madelyn, normally the most tactful of ladies, could not conceal the dismay in her voice. He suspected Miss Coomb's mother was less presentable than her daughter.

At that moment, Miss Coomb arrived in the room with an attractive matron the count assumed was her mother and caused a modest stir among the guests. Naturally, her part in the morning's adventure had made the rounds. He wondered what she had said to Lady Madelyn about his performance. He hoped she did not make his own part in the tale sound *too* heroic. His actions had been rather out of character for a cowardly fop.

"Amelia, my dear," Madelyn said, lifting an imperious hand to summon her friend. "And Mrs. Coomb. Do join us. Count Briccetti, I do not believe you have met Mrs. Coomb."

Andreas rose to his feet and bent over the elder lady's hand.

"I am charmed to meet the mother of such a delightful young lady," he said. "I now perceive the source of her beauty."

Mrs. Coomb simpered in gratification. She was an attractive woman, but her eyes were predatory as she inspected Count Briccetti from the tips of his artfully windswept curls to his soft leather evening slippers. He had chosen the cerulean blue coat and ivory pantaloons deliberately to give the impression of effeminate fragility. This, he suspected, did him no disservice in the eyes of a lady with a marriageable daughter.

Marrying a daughter to the count would be a triumph for any matchmaking mother. That Mrs. Coomb was one of these, he had no doubt.

Miss Coomb was more reserved.

Andreas wondered what had annoyed her most—her mother's unexpected arrival or the inevitable rumors that the attack on Andreas had been precipitated by a jealous husband. He certainly had done all he could to fuel them.

"How are you, Miss Coomb?" he asked. "I would have come to call on you at once, but I thought it wise not to venture out so soon after an attempt was made on my life."

"No doubt the authorities are making every attempt to bring the villain to justice," Lady Madelyn said.

Andreas profoundly hoped not. His superficial friends among the Austrians merely would indulge in a hearty laugh at his expense if they thought he had been accosted by a jealous husband. The more foolish he looked, the better. It would not do for them to suspect the truth.

"Your excellency!" Andreas called out to an Austrian official generally believed to be the true political power in Venice. Field Marshal Felix Bechtold was an intimate of the Archduke Rainer, Viceroy of the Lombard-Veneto Kingdom and the younger brother of Francis I, Emperor of Austria. It was no secret that he made all the most important decisions in Venice during those months the viceroy resided in his other capital of Milan.

The field marshal came over to Andreas at once. He was a tall, athletic, fair-haired gentleman whose gorgeous mustachios identified him as the commanding officer in an Austrian Hussar regiment. He wore his elaborate dress uniform and his many medals and decorations pinned to a wide scarlet sash across his chest with distinction. He was in his late thirties, about the same age as the viceroy.

"My dear count," he said with a solicitude that did not quite conceal the amused contempt in his voice. "I see you have recovered from your little adventure.

All of Venice is abuzz with the incident. We have made inquiries, of course."

"You are too good," the count said. He bowed to the ladies. "If you will excuse us, I feel sure his excellency has questions."

"Can you give me a description of your assailant?" the Austrian asked.

"I think that would be very awkward," Andreas said softly.

The field marshal gave a short burst of laughter.

"I have no doubt," he said shrewdly. "A jealous husband, I gather?"

"I fear it is so," Andreas said with a sigh. "These hotheaded fellows *will* imagine an insult to their women's virtue where none is intended."

"And I suppose there was no justification?"

"Can you doubt it?" Andreas said, sounding aggrieved. "One is obligated to take notice of the ladies. It would be ungallant not to express one's admiration when they go to such pains to please one. But it is the act of a savage to take offense when such innocuous compliments have been paid to one's wife."

"As you say," acknowledged the field marshal, who had an appreciative eye for the ladies himself.

"Listen, my friend," Andreas said, lowering his voice. "Do not pursue the fellow too closely on my account. After all, no harm has been done except to my poor gondolier, who will recover from his superficial wound and be back in my service within the month. So no lasting inconvenience was done. I am a forgiving man."

"Yes." Field Marshal Bechtold stroked his mustachios thoughtfully. "I suppose inquiries might be awkward for you."

"Just so. And for the innocent lady involved."

The field marshal leaned forward.

"Is the lady anyone I would know?" he asked, clearly agog with curiosity.

"Your excellency!" Andreas exclaimed, shocked. "I could never be so . . . ungrateful as to reveal her name."

"Very gallant of you," he said. "Very well. There is no reason to pursue the matter."

Andreas gave him a brilliant smile.

"I knew I could depend on you, my friend. You will come to the little entertainment at my villa on the mainland? It is in your honor."

"I should be delighted." He glanced over to where Amelia Coomb was introducing her obviously bored mother to a group of lady tourists. Unlike Miss Coomb, her mother seemed infinitely more interested in eligible gentlemen than in ladies. "The young lady apparently took no hurt. I think I shall go express my concern."

He smoothed his mustachios and drew himself to his full height. He swaggered over to Amelia and bent over her hand. Her mother's eyes lit with interest.

Andreas frowned.

The fellow had a wife and several children in Austria, but that did not stop him from taking advantage of the cachet that high office gave him in the eyes of the fair sex. To his satisfaction, he saw Lady Madelyn quickly join the group and smoothly take steps to turn the official's attention from Miss Coomb to herself, where it could do no harm with her very attentive husband standing nearby. Andreas knew that as guardian with her husband of four young wards—two of them girls—Lady Madelyn's protective instincts toward innocent young people were finely honed.

There would be no dalliance with Miss Coomb on the part of practiced philanderers while she was under the aegis of Lady Madelyn. On this Andreas could rely.

He had no doubt Lady Madelyn would exert herself to defend the girl from his own attentions as well, now that she knew that he was involved in a dangerous clandestine plot to release his countrymen from Austria's rule.

Pity.

He found the spirited young woman who had emerged from the sad little girl most appealing. But for her own good—and for his—he resolved to keep his distance.

Nine

Amelia's eyes narrowed as she watched Count Andreas Briccetti give a long, languishing look at a tittering lady resplendent in diamonds and egret feathers.

So far, he had spent the entire reception half reclining on a sofa, being lionized by solicitous women. When pressed for details, he had made quite a funny story of his alarms and palpitations at being fired upon by an unknown assailant.

Had those silly women no pride at *all?*

Amelia was absolutely disgusted by the way they competed to bring the count glasses of champagne and dainty little tidbits from the serving tables to help him sustain his strength.

"Look at the silly gudgeon, basking in all the feminine attention," Mr. Langtry observed as he handed Amelia the glass of lemonade he had promised to procure for her.

Amelia couldn't agree more.

"I am sure it is nothing to me if Count Briccetti chooses to waste his time in such a manner," she said.

"Well, there is no harm in him after all," he said tolerantly.

"I thought you disliked him."

Mr. Langtry looked all amazed.

"Dislike Count Briccetti? I? Hardly! How can one

dislike such an ineffectual person?" He lowered his voice and gave a self-conscious laugh. "You are thinking of my fit of jealousy when we came home to find him alone with Madelyn that day. Well, that was simply a misunderstanding. My wife has assured me her friendship with the count is harmless, and I believe her. When one is married to such a spectacular lady, one must expect other men to look in her direction, and not make a fuss about it."

"Lady Madelyn is a remarkable woman," Amelia felt obliged to say, even though she could not like the lady's proprietary manner toward the count.

"Indeed," Mr. Langtry said with a besotted look at his lovely wife. "Not to puff myself up, but I cannot imagine such a strong-minded lady married to a coxcomb such as Count Briccetti. If he has a thought beyond the magnificence of his wardrobe, I would be surprised. Rumor has it he personally oversees his shipping interests, so there must be a brain *somewhere* in his head, for all that he seems at great pains to hide it."

Amelia gave her companion a thoughtful look.

The fashionable fribble Mr. Langtry described certainly did not seem to resemble the man she had met four years ago in Paris. And he certainly had not described the alert, decisive person who unhesitatingly dove into the blue-green waters of the canal to save the life of his wounded gondolier while a gunman remained at large.

"Darling," Mrs. Coomb said breathlessly as she nearly mowed Mr. Langtry down in her zeal to share her news with Amelia. "Oh, I do beg your pardon, Mr. Langtry! I must speak to Amelia at once about a *most* urgent matter."

"Certainly, Mrs. Coomb," the gentleman said politely as he withdrew.

"I have just heard the most distressing thing," Mrs. Coomb said when she had maneuvered her daughter into a corner at the edge of the reception room. "I could not credit my ears."

"What is it, Mother?" Amelia asked, concerned by her mother's obvious agitation.

"The count is to have a Venetian breakfast on Tuesday next at his estate on the mainland. And *you* have declined the invitation."

"Oh, is that all? My note of refusal was *very* polite, I assure you. I am promised to Miss Lorimar for an excursion to Corfu on Friday, and we could not possibly sail to Corfu and return to Venice before the count's party, even if we left today."

"How *can* you place an excursion with an insignificant little ninnyhammer such as Miss Lorimar above an invitation to a Venetian breakfast?"

"Miss Lorimar is *not* a ninnyhammer. And I have been to countless Venetian breakfasts."

"Not in *Venice* you have not! How *could* you disappoint the count?"

"I assure you, he invited me from the merest politeness's sake because I am staying at the British Embassy with his dear friend, Lady Madelyn. He will miss me not at all."

"On the contrary, the count said he is quite desolated that you will not join the party."

Amelia gave a snort of derision.

"He always talks in that overblown style. He means nothing by it."

But Mrs. Coomb, whose hearing was quite selective, was paying no attention to her daughter's protests.

"*Such* a charming and obliging man!" she said rapturously. "It is a fortunate thing that I decided to join you in Venice. You must not make a botch of *this* golden opportunity."

"Golden opportunity?" Amelia exclaimed with great foreboding. "Whatever are you thinking of?"

"Why, the count, of course! He must be at least thirty, and it is past time he was thinking of a wife."

"Mother, you are dreaming of moonshine! *Look* at him." She indicated the count, who was lounging by the fireplace now, laughing at some remark made by one of the women surrounding him. "He does not want for feminine companionship, I assure you."

"But all of those ladies are married, and quite ineligible to become Countess Briccetti. Men will sow their wild oats. A woman of quality ignores them. To carry on his line, he needs *children*. Legitimate children."

"And who better to give them to him than a woman from a foreign country?" Amelia said dryly. "Moreover, one who is far beneath him in fortune and consequence."

"My dear, almost every woman in the polite world is beneath him in fortune and consequence. He is enormously wealthy, and he is accepted in the very highest circles. Most fortunately, he has a taste for English girls. He offered for Lady Madelyn, you know."

"That was more than a year ago."

"Precisely! He's had ample time to turn his thoughts in another direction."

"I am sure the count may turn his thoughts in any direction he pleases with my goodwill. It is nothing whatsoever to do with me."

"Just think what a triumph it would be!" the elder lady exclaimed. Her eyes were sparkling.

"For you or for me?" Amelia asked.

"How can you ask?" Her mother looked hurt. "For you, of course. Everything I have done has been for you."

Amelia would have felt quite chastened if she did not know the truth. Oh, her mother loved her, and with all the single-minded devotion one might expect from a lady who had produced only one child that lived beyond infancy. But the greatest ambition of her life was to make a brilliant match for her daughter, one that would catapult them both into the highest circles in the land.

Amelia had not forgotten that Mrs. Coomb initially rejected dear Quentin's suit for her hand. As a younger son of a prolific family, his fortune and position in society would have been respectable but not nearly important enough to suit Mrs. Coomb's consequence.

After all, her once-insignificant poor relation, Arabella Whittaker, had managed to catch a wealthy viscount for her eldest daughter, and *she,* though a pretty enough girl, had no dowry to speak of. Certainly Violetta Coomb could do as well for *her* daughter.

A titled Venetian nobleman would take the trick nicely.

"I cannot disappoint Miss Lorimar," Amelia said. "It would be most unkind, because on her own she can hardly afford to go to Corfu. She is *so* looking forward to it."

Mrs. Coomb gave a long-suffering sigh.

"The glories of Corfu will still be available *after* the count's party."

Amelia's heart softened at her mother's dejected expression.

Mrs. Coomb might be a shameless social climber, but Amelia couldn't bear to disappoint her either. She was dying to see the inside of the count's villa, and it would be awkward for her to attend without Amelia.

"I will call on Miss Lorimar tomorrow," Amelia said grudgingly. "Perhaps we can go to Corfu another time as easily."

"That is my good girl," Mrs. Coomb said, sailing away to assure the count—as if he had been in doubt, Amelia thought sourly—that Miss Coomb was in transports at the prospect of attending his precious Venetian breakfast and would gladly rearrange her plans to suit his convenience.

By the simple expedient of pasting an ingratiating smile on her face as she elbowed the count's admirers out of her way, Mrs. Coomb soon managed to capture his attention. From the animation on her face and the coquettish little gestures of her fluttering hands, Amelia surmised that her mother was professing her own delight in attending the party. The count, of course, would have been left with no choice but to invite her as well.

To Amelia's embarrassment, the count looked up and caught her looking at him. He smiled at her, and immediately turned to another of the ladies clamoring for his attention. Amelia looked away.

"How fortunate that I find you alone," a deep voice said from behind her. "How are you enjoying your stay in our city?"

"It is lovely, your excellency," she said politely to the viceroy's most trusted friend, Field Marshal Felix Bechtold. He was standing a bit too close for Amelia's comfort, so she stepped back slightly. He promptly followed.

"I should be pleased to show you more of it," he offered. "Perhaps some . . . evening. I should be happy to call for you tomorrow night. The Grand Canal is lovely by moonlight. And we could enjoy a late supper at a trattoria on the piazza."

There was no mistaking his intent. Amelia stifled her sense of outrage and forced a cool note into her voice.

"The Grand Canal is lovely by moonlight, I agree,"

she said. "But my mother is in delicate health, most unfortunately, and susceptible to chills."

"Your mother?" he asked, frowning.

Amelia blinked in surprise.

"Why, your excellency! You did not think I would go on an excursion by moonlight with you if my mother did not accompany us."

"One hears that you were alone with Count Briccetti today when he suffered that unfortunate incident. But then, if there is some understanding between the two of you . . ."

He let his words trail off suggestively.

Apparently, there had been talk about the count and herself, and this man had decided she was fair game for a love affair.

"Not at all," Amelia said, managing to stifle her outrage. "He kindly offered to convey me to the embassy when we met quite by accident at a church he honors with his patronage. The church has some fine paintings, like so many of your lovely churches here, and I was eager to see it."

"If you are fond of paintings, my dear Miss Coomb, I should be pleased to show you about the Doges' Palace. Tintoretto's *Paradise* covers a whole wall of the council chamber and is quite famous. In my personal quarters, I have a fine Venus by Veronese." He had possessed himself of her hand and was idly stroking the palm of it with his thumb. Amelia knew her face was becoming flushed at the intimacy of this touch. "I should enjoy showing it to you tomorrow evening. Your mother could perhaps find some other way to amuse herself. You will be entirely safe with me, I assure you."

Said the fox to the hen, Amelia thought as she tried in vain to withdraw her hand without making her repugnance obvious. She knew that as a guest of the

British Embassy, it would not do for her to insult this politically powerful man. His breath was hot on the side of her face.

From the corner of her eye she saw the count stand and look in their direction. He reached out to capture Lady Madelyn's wrist as she passed by and whispered something in her ear without taking his eyes off Amelia. Lady Madelyn nodded and headed purposefully in Amelia's direction. She could only be relieved.

"How very kind," Amelia said, interrupting the Austrian in his low-voiced recital of pleasures he could provide for her entertainment. "As it happens, I have an engagement for tomorrow evening. Perhaps another time."

"Certainly, Miss Coomb," he said with an insinuating look. "I shall look forward to it."

"As shall I," Amelia said, determined that she would have an impossibly full schedule should he have the effrontery to approach her again.

"Ah, your excellency," said Lady Madelyn as she took the field marshal's arm and smiled up into his eyes. "I have arranged a little musical entertainment in your honor. My husband's ward, Miss Langtry, has agreed to join me in a duet."

"How charming," the gentleman said, and Amelia nearly laughed at the reluctance on his face. While Lady Madelyn's voice was much praised, one could not reasonably expect enduring the warblings of a mere schoolgirl to be anything but a penance.

Because Lady Madelyn left him no choice, however, the field marshal accepted a seat in front of the pianoforte that had been ringed with chairs for the entertainment.

In a lovely gown of peach-hued muslin with ivory lace that made the most of her clear olive complexion, dark, glossy hair, and big brown eyes, Miss Melanie

Langtry looked rather more sophisticated than her tender age of fourteen years would suggest.

She smiled at the company without the least self-consciousness. She obviously had performed often in society. One of Lady Madelyn's friends seated herself at the pianoforte.

Amelia accepted a seat near her mother and prepared herself for a light but competent duet similar to those she had learned as a young girl so she could display her expensively acquired accomplishments in music for the gratification of her social peers.

Her eyebrows rose in real appreciation, though, at the complicated duet of intricate harmonies that Lady Madelyn and Miss Langtry performed. This was no watered-down schoolgirl recital, but a full-blown operatic showpiece. The young girl trilled off the Italian sentences as easily as did Lady Madelyn, whom everyone knew had the benefit of the finest instructors. It appeared she had made the best musical education available to her husband's ward as well.

"Brava!" shouted the count from behind Amelia when the selection was over. *"Molto bella!"*

Lady Madelyn simpered in his direction. Miss Langtry gave him a coquettish little wave of her fingers.

Then the young girl curtsied to the company and went to the stairway, where her brothers and sister, all dressed in formal evening garb, awaited her.

"Let us go into the supper room for refreshment," Lady Madelyn said to the assembled guests as she smoothed Mary Langtry's pretty blond hair and smiled down into the little girl's adoring eyes. She automatically reached out to grab young Matthew, who had a boy's passion for sweets, so he would let the rest of the company pass into the room first.

"We are the hosts, darling," she explained to him. "So we must let our guests precede us."

"I hope they will not snabble all the chocolate eclairs," he said with a pout.

"I had Cook set some back for you, just in case," Lady Madelyn said as she straightened his slightly askew neckcloth. When she spotted Amelia moving toward the end of the group, she let go of the boy and nodded her permission for him and his sister to join the guests in the refreshment suite.

"Amelia, darling. Are you all right?" she asked solicitously.

"Perfectly. Why do you ask?" Amelia could hear the coolness in her own voice.

"There is no reason to be embarrassed. His excellency can be quite forceful when his eye alights on a particular lady. It is a good thing Count Briccetti noticed that he was imposing on you. We had to move the musical entertainment forward a bit to distract him without giving offense, but it worked out well. Perhaps now that we're feeding them early, all these people will go home and we may be comfortable again."

"There has been talk about me, has there not?" Amelia asked.

Lady Madelyn gave a sigh.

"Well, it is inevitable that people will gossip. You *were* alone with the count when his servant was shot."

She gave Amelia a curious look, as if waiting for her to provide information. Did Lady Madelyn suspect the count was interested in her? If so, Amelia would be happy to put her mind at rest.

"It was the merest coincidence that I was visiting a church on one of the other islands when the count was there on some errand. He is the patron of the church, it seems. The gondolier who had taken me to the island was dismissed by mistake, and so the count very kindly offered to convey me back to the city."

"A perfectly rational explanation," Lady Madelyn said approvingly. "That is exactly what you must tell anyone else who asks."

"It happens to be the truth," Amelia insisted.

"Of course, my dear. But an unmarried girl cannot be too careful of her reputation, as I am sure you know. For my own part, I shall be happy to do all I can to discourage talk about the incident."

"How kind," Amelia murmured. It was Lady Madelyn herself who had seemed so determined to bring Amelia to the count's notice. Now she seemed equally determined to distance Amelia from him. What reason could she have for this abrupt about-face except jealousy?

"My dear, have I said something to offend you?" Lady Madelyn asked.

Amelia's conscience smote her. Lady Madelyn had been nothing but generous to her.

"Certainly not," Amelia said as she forced a smile to her lips.

"Then let us go in with the others. I do not know what has become of Robert, and I must keep an eye on Matthew, or he will eat so many sweets that he will be up all night with the stomachache."

"And for Miss Coomb, a lemon tart!" Andreas said as he held the bit of delicate pastry inches from her lips. He had been walking through the group of ladies, impartially offering them tidbits from his plate, so Amelia didn't flatter herself that he was singling her out in particular. It was a silly game—this matching of a lady to her counterpart in confectionery. This one was a strawberry cream; that one was a custard puff.

She was a lemon tart! What was she to make of that?

She should rebuff him. All she had to do was shake her head and refuse the pastry. He would laugh and saunter away to bestow his sweet nothings on some other lady.

Instead, she opened her lips and nibbled a bit of the crust and sweet-tart filling.

"Delicious, is it not?" he said softly.

"Yes. Thank you," she said, taking the rest of the treat from his hands.

"Stay away from his excellency," he warned in an undervoice. "He is a ruthless man."

She raised one eyebrow.

"I am in no danger of succumbing to his overtures, I promise you," she said. "But I thank you for thinking me dimwitted enough to go off with him alone to see his precious Venus by Veronese. In his *personal chambers,* of all things. Does he think me a fool?"

"No. He only hopes," the count said with a smile that didn't reach his eyes. He then moved on to press a candied cherry to the waiting lips of another delighted lady.

Amelia turned away in disgust.

"*There* you are, darling!" her mother said to her. "What did the count say to you?"

"Nothing in particular," Amelia lied.

"I own I was glad to see him approach you. I was afraid your flirtation with the viceroy's subordinate might put him off. He's married, you know."

"I know."

"Pity. Such a handsome man, with such a distinguished figure. But he is a mere nothing compared to the count. He was awarded his present distinction for valor in the late war, I understand, and through the patronage of the viceroy, who finds him an amusing companion, not from any family influence."

"Naturally, a man who elevated himself by his own efforts is to be despised when compared with one who receives every advantage by the simple expedient of being born into the right family and having a fortune that enables him do indulge his every whim."

"Precisely," said her mother, oblivious to all irony when she was engaged in matchmaking. "I hope you did not eat *too* many pastries. Quite bad for the complexion in addition to making one run to fat."

"One would not have thought so from the number of strawberry creams I saw on your plate," Amelia said fondly.

Her mother giggled in response.

"Well, *I* am not on the catch for a husband."

Amelia bit her tongue to keep from saying *she* was not on the catch for a husband either.

Why waste her breath?

Ten

It had rained in the night, and at dawn the whole world from Amelia's balcony window smelled clean and new. She couldn't resist the temptation to explore.

Amelia dressed quickly and stole down the stairs, shoes in hand, to avoid being detained by her mother or her maid.

It was a short walk to the Piazza San Marco from the embassy. Sunrise on the piazza was everything she had hoped, and she stood looking all around her in awe. The sky was streaked with swaths of rose and jade shining through big silver-edged clouds. The rising sun hit the metal on the domes of St. Mark's Basilica and turned them to pure gold.

It was all so lovely—the grand architecture, the cries of vegetable sellers at their booths on the lesser piazzettas, the lapping of the blue-green waters of St. Mark's Basin against the quay. The smell of baking bread wafting from one of the trattorias she passed reminded her that she had neglected to eat breakfast.

No matter.

Amelia would be back in the embassy, tucked back in her bed, by the time her maid knocked on her door to bring her hot chocolate and sweet biscuits with no one the wiser.

She was startled when all this peace was profaned

by the braying of loud laughter carrying quite clearly across the nearly deserted piazza. The unmistakable ringing of male boots against the stone echoed in her ears.

Amelia stepped back into the shadows of the basilica to wait for the men to pass by. She was seen, however; one of them gave a shout and approached her. His companions followed him.

"Come here, pretty one, and tell us your name," one of them called out cheerfully in Italian. He sounded good-natured but drunk. Amelia shrank back in alarm.

"She will not answer you," said an unmistakable voice in the same language. "This little lost kitten is from the English Embassy, and she probably does not understand Italian."

His strong jaw was unshaven, his blond curls were a bit disheveled, and his coat could have used a good pressing, but Amelia had no difficulty recognizing Count Andreas Briccetti, even though she had to squint at him in the glare of the bright morning sun. "I will take her back where she belongs and join you later."

"We will not wait for long. No doubt you and the girl will be detained on the way to the embassy with some joining of a different nature," joked the first man, who gave up his claim of first sighting to the count with good grace.

The men laughed suggestively and proceeded on their way across the square.

"A lost little kitten, am I?" she demanded in English when she and the count were alone.

He burst out laughing.

"Ah, your Italian is better than your French," he observed. "My congratulations."

"Too kind," she murmured. "You are abroad early."

Amelia was not about to tell him that she had made a special study of the language during the past four years because it made her feel connected to the saintly Father Dominic.

"On the contrary, I am seeking my bed late," he said, looking amused. He reached out and cupped her chin with one strong, warm hand and ran a lazy finger across her cheekbone. "You are such a charming innocent."

"Do you mean to say you have been out all night?" she asked, finding it hard to breathe when he was so close. She expected him to reek of sour liquor and sweat after his night's raking, but he smelled of his usual exotic spicy scent.

He shrugged.

"What else is there for me to do with my time?"

"You might stay in your own house at night instead of traversing the city with low company so that assassin might make another attempt on your life."

"Worried about me, Miss Coomb? You need not be. There will be no more attempts." He toyed with the lace trim at the throat of her blue muslin gown. "Did you wear this pretty thing just to greet the morning, or have I interrupted an assignation with one of your admirers?"

Amelia refused to be distracted by this nonsense.

"You know the identity of the man who tried to kill you, then?" she asked as she batted his hand away.

"I feel sure you have heard the rumors that I was accosted by a jealous husband."

"How I miss the man I knew in Paris," she said with a sigh. "He never would have been dishonorable enough to trifle with a married woman."

"That man never existed. Or, if he did, he was playing a part."

"And what part are you playing now?" she asked. "I cannot make you out."

"I?" He made an expansive gesture with his hands. "I am the simplest of men to comprehend. It amused me to make a pet of you in Paris, so I did. Here, in Venice, it amuses me to stay out all night with my friends, so I do. I am the very soul of consistency."

"I see now I was quite mistaken in crediting you with any noble qualities whatsoever," she said archly.

He made her an extravagant bow.

Amelia smiled as he took her hand and led her toward the Doges' Palace to reach the promenade along the Grand Canal. She paused to look back at the piazza. Droplets of water clinging to the stones made them dazzle the eye like diamonds in the sun. She craned her neck back to admire the four great bronze horses above the portal of the great basilica. They had been forged in Nero's Rome, Amelia had learned from a guidebook, and brought in triumph to Venice during the Fourth Crusade.

Her senses were overcome by the beauty and color of it all.

"If you think this is wonderful," he said, reading her thoughts, "you should see the piazza in December, dusted with snow. It is my favorite time of year, when the tourists have all gone home and the city is mine. But you would find it too cold and wet."

"Cold and wet? I am *English,* Count Briccetti. There is nothing you or Venice may teach me of cold and wet, although, as a rule, I would not go out of my way to seek it."

"I stand corrected," he said with a smile at her tart tone.

"Thank you for coming to my rescue just now," she said. It was impossible to remain out of charity with him for long. "It might have been . . . awkward without your intervention."

"It is my very great pleasure," he said, smiling warmly. "I shall escort you to the embassy now, if you are ready."

"Certainly. It was foolish of me to come alone, but I wanted to see the piazza at dawn and feared I would have no other opportunity. Neither my mother nor Lady Madelyn is an early riser."

"Sometimes the Langtry children's nurse brings them early to the square in the company of a sturdy footman for protection. You might ask if you can accompany them if you wish to come again."

"You certainly are familiar with the habits of Lady Madelyn's family."

"We are old friends, as you know," he said.

"And lovers?"

He gave her speculative look.

"That is the gossip."

"Is it the truth?" When he did not answer, she averted her eyes. "You remind me, quite rightly, that it is none of my business."

"No, it is not," he agreed with perfect good humor.

They walked on in silence for several moments while Amelia looked all about her. The Doges' Palace was all pink stone and graceful archways that gave a feeling of airiness to a building the size of a small city.

"I adore this place," she murmured in appreciation. "Have you seen the lovely little marble bridge palace that spans the Rio di Palazzo? It is so romantic."

"It is called the Bridge of Sighs," he said grimly, "because it connects the Doges' Palace with a prison from which few emerged alive during the days of the republic. Casanova, the great lover, was one of the few prisoners to escape from it, and he did not find the experience romantic in the least, I assure you."

"Oh. I had not known," she said, digesting this. It quite ruined her imaginative fancy of lovers strolling the bridge, hand in hand.

When they arrived on the steps of the embassy, the count clasped her hand for a moment. "Good morning to you, my dear. And take care. This is not so romantic or so kind a city to strangers as it seems."

"How lovely it is!" said Miss Lorimar as she and Amelia disembarked from the boat that had brought them to the mainland where the patricians of the old Republic of Venice had built so many of their summer homes. She had been so pleased to escape from her brother and sister-in-law's lively children when Amelia invited her to accompany her on the short excursion. You would have thought her sister-in-law had presented her with a pocketful of diamonds instead of merely having granted her permission to leave her responsibilities as family drudge for a few hours. "Oh, look at the villas on the hill! Are they not sumptuous?"

Amelia nodded absently at her friend's cheerful observation as she sought in vain for a way to beg off from the trip to Corfu.

Miss Lorimar—who seemed to be memorizing each blade of grass, each flower, each shaft of sunlight—had a great ambition to travel the world but, alas, not the means to indulge it.

Her fond brother and his wife would have been hurt to the quick if anyone had suggested that Miss Lorimar was not perfectly happy with them or that she might want something more out of life than to be a cheerful domestic slave for her sister-in-law and her three lively children.

Neither her brother nor her sister-in-law, for instance, had asked Miss Lorimar whether *she* wanted to go on a whirlwind tour of Italy, although if they *had* asked her, she certainly would have expressed herself willing enough to go. As Mr. and Mrs. Lorimar congratulated themselves on their generosity to their dependent sister, it apparently didn't occur to them that she might not want to spend all her time in the nursery rooms of their rented house supervising the children while her benefactors enjoyed themselves.

What else had she to do with her time after all?

Amelia knew her friend's particular romantic taste leaned toward ancient Greece, and the proposed excursion to Corfu was of great importance to her. She had been thrilled when her brother and sister-in-law graciously granted her permission to go.

The young ladies' unspoken understanding that Amelia would pay the boat fare and lodging for the trip while Miss Lorimar paid for her own personal expenses out of the pittance of an allowance her brother bestowed upon her made it possible for her to go without losing face.

Amelia had made a point of stressing what a great favor Miss Lorimar had done her by agreeing to keep her company on her little holiday. Thus Miss Lorimar could accept what amounted to charity and keep her pride intact.

That was why what Amelia needed to tell her would be so difficult.

Especially since Miss Lorimar herself brought up the subject of Corfu at every opportunity.

"I was able to find a pair of stout boots in my size at one of the shops yesterday at a bargain price, am I not fortunate? My dear brother insisted upon giving them to me as a gift. He is so kind to me! So, I am all ready for our little adventure."

"Loralee—"

"My sister-in-law asks if she should have her cook prepare a hamper of food for us to take along. If there is food for sale on the ship, she says we may depend upon it that it is dreadfully dear—"

"Loralee—"

"I say, Amelia," Miss Lorimar said. Her brow was furrowed as a thought occurred to her. "Do you think we will be obliged to tip the pilot of the ship? If so, how much do you think—"

"Loralee!" Amelia shouted in frustration.

Miss Lorimar blinked once, then smiled apologetically.

"Oh, my dear Amelia. I am so sorry for babbling on and on without letting you get a word in! It would serve me right if you decided you couldn't bear the company of such an addlepot for the duration of a trip to Corfu. I am just so excited, but you have my complete attention now. What is it you wish to tell me?"

"I don't know how to tell you this," Amelia said in despair.

Miss Lorimar's face fell.

"You are not going to Corfu?" she said slowly.

"I find I have a pressing engagement on Tuesday next," Amelia admitted. She hated herself for her relief that Miss Lorimar had guessed and she had not been obliged to grope for a way to break the bad tidings to her. "One I can't break or postpone. But it is no great matter, after all. We may still go to Corfu if we leave on Wednesday next rather than Friday. Surely that will do as well."

"No, I'm afraid it will not." Miss Lorimar tried to smile and failed abysmally. Tears of disappointment welled in her eyes. She turned away in a vain attempt to hide them. "My brother and his wife have engaged to leave for Florence the week after that. That is why you and I agreed to leave on Friday."

"Oh, yes. I remember now," Amelia said, feeling even worse. "I am so very sorry, Loralee. I know you were looking forward to the trip. But I have received an invitation to Count Briccetti's villa, and my mother is adamant that I should go—"

Miss Lorimar smiled bravely.

"I certainly know the pressures that one's relations—well intentioned though they may be—*will* bring to bear on one."

"I am so very sorry," Amelia said again.

Her companion gave her hand a squeeze.

"Think nothing of it, Miss Coomb."

Amelia was Miss Coomb again.

That Miss Coomb and Miss Lorimar were on Christian-name terms was mere condescension on the part of Miss Coomb, and Miss Lorimar's reverting to the more formal form of address underlined this.

"Oh, Loralee," Amelia said with a regretful sigh when she saw her friend's shoulders shake with the effort of suppressing her sobs.

"This is so silly of me," Miss Lorimar said with a bright smile. She must have had a lot of practice denying her true feelings to placate those upon whose whim she depended for the very food she ate and the roof over her head. "I don't know what has come over me. After all, I have another month in Italy with my brother and his family before I must go home to England. Florence, I understand, is very sunny and beautiful. Have you been there, Miss Coomb?"

"No, I have not," Amelia replied. "Listen, Loralee. I will explain to my mother that it is impossible for me to go to Count Briccetti's Venetian breakfast."

"You are going to a Venetian breakfast at the count's villa? A *real* one?"

"It is of no consequence whatsoever," Amelia said. The wistfulness on Miss Lorimar's face cut her to the quick. "I can refuse."

"No! I will not let you make such a sacrifice for my sake!" Loralee exclaimed.

"But—"

"The fact that you would even suggest it shows how good a friend you are to me. Not another word," she said when Amelia would have insisted. She took a deep shuddering breath and gave Amelia a brave attempt at a smile. "Do you smell that? Those must be lemon trees. Have you ever smelled such a clean, pleasing fragrance?"

"No," Amelia said, torn between guilt and affection. "It is quite delightful."

A thought occurred to her.

"I have an idea. Let us go back to the city and have some pastries at that little shop on the Rialto Bridge," she suggested. "My treat. I insist."

"What a *wicked* extravagance," Loralee exclaimed, although her expression was hopeful. "Dare we?"

"Of course we dare. We *deserve* it if we are to be denied Corfu," Amelia said, abundantly aware that she was trying to pacify her friend with sweets as if she were a disappointed child.

But if Loralee felt condescended to, she did not show it.

"Very well," she said, "but I shall want one of those custard cream puffs with chocolate and a candied cherry on top, the kind that oozes all over one's nose and chin when one bites into it."

"Let's have *two* each," Amelia said recklessly.

If she split the seams in her new, never-before-worn jonquil yellow promenade dress, the one with the white and ice blue ribbons that her mother insisted she must wear to the count's Venetian breakfast, she didn't care.

Eleven

Count Andreas Briccetti's summer villa on the mainland was the crowning jewel of a countryside full of jewels, and for the afternoon of the Venetian breakfast it was transformed into a pleasure palace.

Great billowy tents of jade green and peach silk were raised to the skies to shelter serving tables groaning with every delicacy imaginable. For the guests' comfort, soft pillows and priceless Oriental rugs were spread all about the floors of the three-sided tents. Musicians playing violins and flutes strolled among the guests.

And the count himself, resplendent in a blue coat and wearing a wide-brimmed straw hat that did not make him look in the least like a rustic, went from party to party, making his guests feel welcome. He carried a great bouquet of yellow roses, and presented each lady—young or old—with a fresh bloom upon arrival.

"How charming," Lady Madelyn said as she accepted one and sniffed it delicately. "It will do none of us the least credit to have a party in Venice for the rest of the season after this. As usual, you have outdone us all."

"Have I, my dear?" he said archly. "You relieve my

mind. Miss Coomb?" He held out a rose to her and she accepted it.

"Thank you," she whispered.

He was quite daunting today, despite his genial manner.

The Venetian breakfast was supposed to resemble a country entertainment, although no one seemed to know whether it actually originated in Venice. But the number of servants present, the lavish villa in the background, the yellow roses that would not be in season for at least another month, and the fact that all of the aristocracy of Venice and the highest ranking officials of the Austrian occupational government seemed to be present when one would suppose they had more pressing engagements in the middle of the day only underlined the fact that the count was as remote from Amelia in situation as one of the royal dukes.

"Is this not divine?" Mrs. Coomb asked with a sigh of pleasure as she settled onto one of the cushions. Amelia could see her smugness at being flexible enough to recline on the carpets instead of having to avail herself of a chair like some of the more elderly guests whose arthritic limbs did not permit them to do so.

At present the count was sprawled picturesquely on a slight hill, permitting one of his many laughing admirers to feed him grapes by hand.

Amelia knew exactly where he was at every given moment. It was as if her awareness were perfectly attuned to him.

"Lobster patties!" her mother said, giving Amelia a significant look as she accepted one of the delicacies from the platter of a liveried servant. "How delightful."

Amelia knew Mrs. Coomb believed an abundance

of lobster patties—especially at what was supposedly a casual afternoon entertainment—was an infallible indication of a host's wealth and status.

"I am so pleased you are not gorging yourself like all the other young ladies present," Mrs. Coomb said, patting Amelia on the hand. "It makes one look so *greedy*. But do try to smile more, dearest."

Obligingly, Amelia smiled at her.

"Forgive me, Mother. I am afraid I am not good company today. I keep thinking of poor Miss Lorimar, having to forgo her excursion because of me."

"Well, I am sure your concern for your friend does credit to your tender heart, but it was out of the question for you to decline the count's invitation."

"Mother, he doesn't even know I am here."

"Of course he does. He greeted you very prettily and gave you a flower. There is always a special softness in his eye when he looks at you. A mother can tell these things."

Amelia rolled her eyes.

"He looks at all the other ladies exactly the same way," Amelia told her, knowing that she might as well save her breath.

"Yes. That is only to throw the gossips off." But Mrs. Coomb's eyes were twinkling, and Amelia had to laugh. Her mother knew very well that she was being outrageous, and one of the things Amelia loved most about her was her ability to laugh at herself.

Amelia caught the eye of Lady Madelyn, who had been smiling prettily into the eyes of Field Marshal Felix Bechtold. She held the Austrian off firmly when he would have put his arms around her to lead her into the dance, made her excuses to him, and came to join Amelia and her mother.

Lady Madelyn was still smiling, but her eyes held the residue of impatience in them.

"Is this not the most delightful party! I wonder where Robert has got to," she said, looking around.

"Like our host, he probably is lying on cushions somewhere, being fed grapes by odalisques," Amelia said. That came out rather more tartly than she intended.

Lady Madelyn looked in the direction of Amelia's gaze and pursed her lips at the spectacle of the count biting into a red grape being held aloft by a laughing young lady in a green dress.

"He had better *not* be," she said with narrowed eyes. Then she smiled at Mrs. Coomb and Amelia. "Forgive me. I am not at my best in strong sunlight. It always gives me the headache. Amelia, dear, if you do not mind, will you accompany me to the house? If I know Count Briccetti, he has a lovely, cool little room equipped with lavender water and attentive maids tucked away somewhere for just this purpose. If you will pardon my saying so, you look a bit flushed as well."

"Yes, Amelia, do go with Lady Madelyn and have a nice rest. You know how delicate you are," said Mrs. Coomb.

Delicate, indeed! Amelia was nothing of the kind. But her fond mother persisted in the notion that a pale, delicate lady was somehow more refined than one who, like Amelia, enjoyed rude good health at all seasons.

Amelia had no objection to having an excuse to see the inside of Count Briccetti's villa, however, so she eagerly accepted Lady Madelyn's invitation.

They traversed a short run of marble stairs to an archway of pink stone similar to that of the Doges' Palace. A dark coolness descended upon their heated skin immediately when they passed inside.

Lady Madelyn gave a sigh of relief.

"Thank goodness," she said. "Another moment out on the lawn and I might have started to *freckle.*"

"A catastrophe of no mean order," Amelia agreed. There was no irony in her tone, for she, too, was prone to the unsightly blotches across the bridge of her nose if she did not take care.

Lady Madelyn lifted a graceful hand to her brow.

"Ah. There is a servant." She asked the servant, in Italian, if the count had arranged for a room in which the ladies could retire. The servant ushered them at once to a beautiful, airy room furnished with several couches covered in pillows and white linen around a sunken pool of smooth pink and white tiles. Lily blossoms and rose petals floated in the water. Low tables covered in blue silk drapery held bowls of artistically arranged pears, apples, grapes, and peaches.

"I adore my husband. Never doubt it, Amelia. But at times like this," Lady Madelyn said with a mischievous smile, "I do wonder if I was quite in my right mind when I refused the count's proposal. Have you ever seen anything so deliciously decadent?"

"Never," Amelia said as she helped Lady Madelyn remove her pretty white lace gown so she would be more comfortable. A smiling servant hung it up. Lady Madelyn, now wearing a lavishly embroidered white chemise and petticoat, lay down on one of the couches and closed her eyes. Her brow was furled as if she were in pain.

The headache, Amelia realized, was real. She had half suspected that Lady Madelyn merely invented it as a pretext to explore the house.

"Lavender water or vinegar?" Amelia asked as she picked up a white cloth and moved to a table containing silver ewers of the two liquids.

"Lavender, please," Lady Madelyn said, smiling gratefully at her. She gave a sigh of pleasure when

Amelia pressed the cloth to her forehead. "Thank you. Now I shall close my eyes and try to sleep for a bit."

Amelia thought about doing the same, but she felt quite restless now that she was out of the sunlight. She bent over the pool and allowed the silken, perfumed water to trail from her fingers. She wiped her hands on the towel an attentive servant held out to her and helped herself to a peach so ripe the sweet juice dripped down her chin.

Lady Madelyn opened one eye.

"My dear, I can hear you fidgeting. You need not stay with me. I would not wish for you to miss the party for my sake."

"I do not mind," Amelia said politely, if not with perfect truth.

"I am not an invalid. Go! If I need anything, I will ask one of the servants. And when you go back to the party, you might find Robert and tell him where I am, if you would be so obliging."

"Certainly. I shall be happy to do so."

"That would be very kind," Lady Madelyn said drowsily. "Do you think you can find your way outside again?"

"Of course I can," Amelia said, but after turning through one hall after another, she had no idea where she was. And she didn't care.

Each new room of Count Briccetti's palace was as beautiful as the last. The Ca' Briccetti on the Grand Canal was magnificent; it was an impressive monument to the count's wealth and prestige. But to Amelia's taste, this villa was even more attractive. It seemed built not to impress, but to refresh the heart and soul.

The ceilings were high and decorated with elaborate moldings in the forms of wreaths and flowers. The floors were inlaid tiles in delicate colors of rose and green and white. Sumptuous paintings of classical gods and goddesses decorated the walls except for a few conspicuous places where the niches were empty.

Amelia had heard that Napoleon demanded many of the city's treasures as a bribe in exchange for sparing Venice the outrages he and his troops inflicted on other conquered cities. It appeared that the House of Briccetti had borne part of the price of this restraint.

From the appearance of this villa, however, it was apparent that he had much wealth left.

Amelia passed into a narrow hallway and came face-to-face with a life-size marble statue that caused her to blush. The stone maiden was of Amelia's own height. A wreath of sculpted roses adorned her flowing marble hair—and that was the extent of the maiden's raiment except for a few fading caresses of the colored paint that must have decorated the statue when it was new. The well-shaped lips, though pale, were so beautifully molded, they seemed to be of living flesh.

Amelia never had seen anything like it. She stepped forward for a closer look and traced the lovely face with a reverent finger. She wondered how old it was, and felt a little sad at the thought that when she was old and wrinkled, this maiden would still be young and beautiful.

She smiled with self-mockery.

What a morbid thought for such a beautiful day.

At the statue's back was a bubbling fountain and a wooden door with a rounded top that was half concealed by an abundant flowering plant in a stone pot. At its feet was a faded but still beautiful Oriental carpet.

Amelia's curiosity was piqued by the door, but she heard the low drone of several male voices coming from behind it and good manners forbade her to intrude.

She was about to turn from the maiden and make her way outside, when a passionate voice rang out.

"Are we dogs or women, to cower under the lash of our masters?"

The Italian words were pregnant with danger. The speaker was answered by a calm, deliberate voice.

His.

"I have told you never to come here. You must leave at once before someone sees you," said the count.

"Yes. We must not disturb your guests while they are feasting on the life's blood of our citizens."

Even a person with an imperfect command of the language could not miss the sarcasm.

"This would be the perfect opportunity. To kill Field Marshal Bechtold, the viceroy's good friend, while he lies there, gorging his fat face with fruits and little cakes," the count's adversary continued.

"We are close—so close—to success. You will *not* destroy everything with an act of foolish bloodshed."

"The Austrian dog must die!"

"And if he does, they will send someone worse in his place."

"But they will know that we are men, not slaves to bare our necks so they may place their heels upon them! I will eat out his heart."

Amelia started to back away. She had stumbled upon a conspiracy, one not meant to be overheard.

Count Briccetti's voice was a steel blade of menace.

"Then you will die of indigestion, my hotheaded friend."

Before she could get away, her foot caught on an edge of the Oriental carpet and she gave an involuntary gasp that seemed too loud to her own ears as she stumbled against the potted plant.

A muttered oath sounded from behind her.

Suddenly, an angry, dark-haired man burst through

the door, grabbed Amelia, and propelled into a small room as he cruelly twisted her arm up behind her.

"Let me go," she cried out in English.

Four strangers regarded her with varying emotions, most of them deadly. The count merely looked amused.

"Let go of the girl. You are frightening her," the count said in Italian with a genial smile as he came to Amelia's side.

When her captor released her, the count took her abused arm and gave it a slow, intimate caress.

"He did not hurt you, did he?" he asked her in English. The smile didn't leave his lips, but there was a warning in his eyes.

"No," she said, staring at him. Her throat was so dry, she could barely croak the word.

Who *was* this man?

He certainly was not the kind priest who comforted her in Paris when she was desperate and hurting.

He was not the urbane courtier who set the ladies' hearts aflutter here in Venice.

Nor was he the self-indulgent buffoon who inspired contempt among less-favored men.

This man, though he wore Count Briccetti's clothes and smiled out of his face, wore an aura of menace.

"She heard us. She heard everything," her captor said in Italian. "She must die."

"And where," the count inquired in the same language as he continued to smile at Amelia, "do you plan to conceal all of these corpses? Not on *my* land. Not when I have been at such pains to demonstrate that my house is always open to our Austrian friends."

He laughed indulgently and put his arm around Amelia. He placed a nibbling kiss at her ear.

"Look at her!" he said in a contemptuous voice.

"The stupid little cow does not understand a word we are saying."

"Then why was she standing outside the room, listening to us?"

"She was not listening to us, you fool. She had thrown off her dragon of a mother and was looking for me." He stroked Amelia's hair as if she were some sort of pet and slowly, insinuatingly, traced his thumb across her collarbone. She was so frightened, her breath caught in her throat and her eyes started to flutter closed. He addressed his next sentence to her in English. "My sweet girl cannot get enough of me, can you, my pet?"

She tried to struggle out of his embrace, but a band of steel clamped her to his side.

He cupped her cheek in one hand to force her to look into his face, and she understood the message of his eyes.

Do not speak. Do not struggle. Your life depends on it.

"I will take care of your needs when I am rid of this rabble," he whispered in English as he boldly traced the top of her bosom with his hand and allowed it to trail down the side of one breast.

He released her, and she felt her knees start to buckle.

The count laughed softly and grasped her around the waist. He placed a warm kiss on the side of her exposed neck.

"She has seen our faces," her captor rapped out. "She must die."

Amelia recognized his voice as the one who had demanded the death of the field marshal.

"What a waste," the count said insinuatingly in Italian as he traced the edge of Amelia's ear with his finger. "Look at this pretty face. I can silence her, and much more effectively than you can." His voice deepened. "She is my slave. She will forget your existence a moment after I take her to my bed."

"She is a spy!"

The count burst out laughing.

"Nonsense. The girl has a brain the size of a flea." He fondled her again. "And a body eager for love. She is harmless."

"Harmless!" the other spat out. "She could mean the death of all of us."

"She *will* mean the death of all of us if she is killed. *Think,* my hotheaded fool! She is the guest of the British ambassador and the protégée of Lady Madelyn. Do you think there would not be a thorough investigation into her death? Or that every stone in Venice will not be overturned if she is found missing?"

He gave her a contemptuous smile.

"Believe me," he said disdainfully, "she is not worth the trouble of killing. I will have my sport with her and she will go home with her mother. She will not give your presence here another thought. Now go. I do not want any of the other guests to see you."

Amelia sagged in his arms when the men left.

"Steady, my girl," he said just under his breath as he held her close for a moment. "You are safe. You did well."

She pulled herself together and pushed him away.

"Yes, for a stupid little cow with the brain of a flea," she retorted.

"I was afraid you understood that," he said ruefully.

"Hot for you, am I? Your *slave,* am I?" she cried. "How *dare* you say such disgusting things about me?"

"Softly, my dear. Softly," he warned. "I did it to save your beautiful hide, Miss Coomb."

"Who are they?"

"They are desperate men, and but for me you would

be dead now and your body stored in the cellar, awaiting burial at nightfall in my vineyard in the hills."

He said it with a conviction that made gooseflesh burst forth on her arms.

"Listen to me," he said earnestly. "They must never know you understood what they were saying. You must take care. Our spies are in the British Embassy. And outside it, they will be watching you now that they have reason to fear you could expose us."

"What terrible thing are you mixed up in?"

"Freedom from our oppressors," he said. "My men are loyal but impatient."

"They were plotting to kill the field marshal."

"No. This I will not allow," he said harshly. "His death will only make the Austrians squeeze us harder. The only way to remove their yoke from our shoulders is to enlist the support of foreign powers."

"Such as England," she said slowly. No wonder he had been dancing attendance on the British delegation. "I don't suppose Lady Madelyn has been active in the negotiation for support for your cause in the most unofficial of capacities. Who would suspect she received you alone in her husband's absence merely to talk of toppling the government?"

"Ah, my dear Amelia," he said approvingly. "So intelligent. *Do* hide it at all costs. Your life, and mine, may depend upon it."

"What must I do?" she asked.

"You must go back to the embassy with your mother and arrange to return to England at once. I can provide transport for you on one of my ships if need be. They will not pursue you there."

"But what about you?"

"I? I will stay here and play out my part."

"Men!" Amelia said on the verge of tears. "Always so eager to die for political causes."

"Will you worry about me, Amelia?" he asked with a fond smile.

"Of course I will, you foolish man! All this time I was despising you for flirting with Lady Madelyn and all those other ladies, and now I *wish* that is all you were up to."

He gently took her into his embrace and allowed her to rest her head on his chest. She drew in a long, shuddering breath.

"It is selfish of me," he said, "but it pleases me that you will care if I lose my life in this cause. I don't think anyone else will. They will be too busy fighting over the spoils."

"Hah! What about all your lady friends?"

"Them least of all," he said. "Now. Will you do as I ask? Will you leave Venice at once?"

She nodded because she was too overcome to speak.

Once she left Venice, she would never see him again.

"Be careful." She could barely croak out the words.

"And you, Amelia," he said. "I have been too long away from my guests. I will escort you to the ladies' withdrawing room. It might be well if you would cultivate a small indisposition to set the stage for your return to England. After a few moments you can return to the party with one of the other ladies resting there. I do not think we should invite gossip by returning together."

"Yes. Of course," she said, taking the arm he offered.

"It would be well if you would stay in plain view, preferably in the company of Sir Gregory or Lady Madelyn and her husband until you return to the embassy. Their presence will keep you safe. No more going off alone to explore, no?"

"No," she said. "I promise."

They went back through the halls in silence. There did not seem to be anything more to say.

At the doorway to the withdrawing room, he smiled sadly and held both of her hands for a moment.

"Farewell, my dear Miss Coomb," he whispered. "Be happy when you return to your life in England. Be safe."

Twelve

Lady Madelyn was sipping a cup of tea from a dainty porcelain cup when Amelia entered the ladies' withdrawing room.

"You look quite restored," Amelia said, trying to smile at her and failing. She was not sure how she felt about the woman who was involved with Count Briccetti's dangerous attempt to overthrow the Austrians.

Lady Madelyn's brows came together in concern.

"That is more than what I can say for you, my dear," she said, rising and putting her arm around Amelia. "You look as if you have been crying. Are you unwell?"

She started to deny it, but remembered that she was to cultivate an indisposition as a pretext for leaving Venice.

"Yes, but pray do not mention it to Mama. I do not want to spoil her enjoyment of the party."

"You poor dear," she said. "If you wish to go back to the embassy now, I will find Robert and—"

"No, I would not dream of spoiling your outing. I shall be perfectly all right in a moment."

"Very well," Lady Madelyn said, looking relieved. "We will go back to the party when you are ready."

The rest of the afternoon passed in a blur for Amelia.

"Darling, do have another of these lobster patties," her mother urged her. "They are *so* delicious. And this wine, and the white grapes. Oh, Venice is the most delightful place!"

Amelia forced a smile to her face and took a grape. The juice was so sweet, and the sunshine was so bright and beautiful.

The musicians, dressed in colorful peasant costumes, played a lively tune, and couples danced with cheerful abandon. The count went from group to group, and she often saw his golden head thrown back in laughter.

Lady Madelyn, more often than not, was the one laughing with him.

But it was all a mockery.

Beneath the surface, Venice was a powder keg about to explode in rebellion.

And Andreas was at its center.

Later, at the embassy, Mrs. Coomb's face fell with disappointment when Amelia told her that she wanted to go home to England.

"But, love. I have only just arrived," she protested. "Surely this trifling indisposition of yours will pass."

Amelia gave a sigh of frustration. Much as her fond mother wished to convey the impression to society that Amelia was a delicate flower, she was not inclined to cosset her now, not when the elder lady was enjoying Venice so much. It was a grand coup for the socially ambitious Mrs. Coomb to be the guest of the British Embassy. In fact, Lady Madelyn had not invited Mrs. Coomb to join them in Venice; Mrs. Coomb merely sailed for Venice and trusted that Lady Madelyn's good manners would compel her to accept the fait accompli with good grace.

If Amelia went home to England, Mrs. Coomb had no excuse whatsoever to remain in Venice and enjoy a level of society to which she had aspired all her adult life. She was not about to surrender this advantage through some nonsense of her provoking daughter's!

She patted Amelia's hand.

"A good night's sleep will put you to rights, my dear. You will be quite yourself again in the morning, I promise you."

For the next two days Amelia declined all invitations and lay listlessly in her bed and pretended to be ill.

On the third day, Count Briccetti called at the embassy to express his concern. Amelia hastily donned a morning gown in blue muslin and fidgeted as her maid dressed her hair. This process was delayed by her mother's supervision. Mrs. Coomb was eager for her daughter to appear at her best advantage for a visit from the count.

Despite Amelia's discouragement, Mrs. Coomb still cherished the hope of making a marriage for her daughter that would inspire all of London's aristocratic circles with jealousy.

"Good afternoon, Count Briccetti," Amelia said after her mother was finally satisfied with her appearance and she was permitted to join Lady Madelyn and their visitor in the parlor. He stood and offered her a bouquet of yellow roses. She accepted it and buried her nose in the fragrant blooms. "How very kind of you," she said. She was mortified by the way her voice quavered, but she supposed it would add credence to her pretense of illness.

At Lady Madelyn's nod, the servant who had just laid out tea and cakes on a small refreshment table took the roses to put them in water.

"I hope you are feeling better, my dear?" said Lady Madelyn as she drew Amelia over to the sofa with the apparent intention of seating her between herself and the count.

"Yes, thank you," Amelia said as she sat. The count sat as well, but before Lady Madelyn could resume her own seat on the sofa, Mrs. Coomb took a hand in the matter.

"I think there is nothing wrong with my daughter that a bit of fresh air would not cure," Mrs. Coomb suggested as she sat on the count's other side, thus crowding Amelia and the count together and effectively making the sofa too crowded for four persons.

With a good grace, Lady Madelyn took a seat opposite them.

"Perhaps a ride in a gondola. Or a walk to the piazza for an Italian ice," Mrs. Coomb said with a look of appeal at the count.

Amelia blushed crimson at her mother's idea of subtlety.

"Nothing would please me more than to escort you both," he said with a disarming smile, "but, most unfortunately, I have a pressing engagement this afternoon."

"Of course," Amelia said.

"Lady Madelyn tells me you wish to go home, Miss Coomb," he said pointedly. "I would be delighted to offer you transport on one of my ships. One of them leaves for England tomorrow."

"How excessively kind," she said with a grateful smile. "I should be happy to accept—"

"My dear count," Mrs. Coomb interrupted with a pretty, artificial laugh. "Your concern for my daughter's health is most gratifying, but she would not *dream* of disappointing Lady Madelyn when she has been so kind to her."

"But, Mother, I—"

"*I* would not dream of allowing Miss Coomb to

stay on my account when she is unwell," Lady Madelyn said. "Let us consider the matter settled."

"Thank you both," Amelia said, trying not to resent Lady Madelyn and Count Briccetti's apparent collusion to get rid of her.

But Mrs. Coomb was not about to be beaten.

"Nonsense! As her mother, I can be depended upon to know what is best for Amelia," Mrs. Coomb said with a playful wag of her finger at her daughter. "It does not do to humor these young girls' crotchets, you know.

"Not," she added hastily for the count's benefit, "that my darling Amelia is not as a rule the most accommodating girl imaginable. She has never given me a moment's trouble in her upbringing, I assure you."

Amelia observed the cynical glint in the count's eye and wished the floor would open and the earth swallow her up. He knew very well that her mother had set her heart on catching him as a husband for Amelia, the odiously conceited man! Well, he would not have remained a bachelor for so long if he were not adept at frustrating the ambition of many a matchmaking mama.

"You look flushed, Amelia," Lady Madelyn suggested. "I do hope you are not feverish."

Amelia was about to seize gratefully upon this idea, but her mother merely tut-tutted it away.

"Certainly not," Mrs. Coomb said with a little trill of laughter. "She would not *dare* be ill for the archduke's ball tomorrow night. We are quite looking forward to it, are we not, my love?"

"Yes, Mama," Amelia murmured. "That is, we *were*, until—"

"So, do not worry," Mrs. Coomb said to the count. "Amelia will save at least two dances, one of them a waltz, for you."

"You quite relieve my mind," he said.

The poor man. What else *could* he say?

"But, Mama, I—"

"Hush, my dear," Mrs. Coomb said with a wide smile that belied the hard glare in her eyes as she stared at her daughter. "You may depend upon your mother to know what is best for you."

"Yes, Mama," she murmured.

"Now I must leave you," the count said as he rose from the sofa. Amelia stood with the other ladies, but she was so mortified, she could not look him in the face when he took her hand.

"I shall look forward to seeing you at the ball," he said, but he didn't sound happy about it. "If you should change your mind and wish to return to England after all—"

"She won't," Mrs. Coomb said firmly.

Her smile hardened along the edges as soon as the count turned away with Lady Madelyn, who, in her role as hostess, accompanied him to the foyer.

"Come along with me, missy," Mrs. Coomb hissed as her hand fastened talonlike to her daughter's wrist. She led her straight up to her room and, Amelia felt sure, would have slammed the door with a resounding crash if she had dared.

Amelia prepared herself for a tremendous scold and gaped at her mother when that lady gave a trill of triumphant laughter and clutched Amelia to her bosom.

"My darling, you are a genius!" she cried. She abruptly released her and opened the wardrobe. "Yellow roses! The man is positively *mad* for you!" She frowned at Amelia. "Do not let your mouth hang open like that, dearest. It is *most* unbecoming."

"But, Mama—"

"I must admit, I was quite vexed with you for languishing in your bed with the vapors, but it has answered the purpose delightfully! The rose brocade for tomorrow, do you not agree, love?"

"He already has seen it, unfortunately, but it *has* been some time, so—what am I saying? Mama, I am *not* going to the ball. I am too ill."

"None of that, my girl! That answered delightfully the past few days, but now it is time to follow up your advantage." She gave a satisfied sigh. "I suppose we cannot arrange the wedding yet this spring, and most of the ton will have left London by summer, but we can have the wedding in Brighton. Perhaps the King himself will attend!"

"Mama, you are aiming at the moon!"

"So you have said before, my dear," Mrs. Coomb said with a playful wag of her forefinger, "and now you will see that you are wrong."

Andreas had left instructions with his steward to convey any message from the British Embassy to him immediately in the forlorn hope that Amelia or Lady Madelyn would write to accept his offer of passage for Amelia and her mother to England on his ship, but he had to admit defeat when eight o'clock arrived and it was time for his valet to embark upon the elaborate preparation of the count's person for the ball.

It was to be held at the Doges' Palace and hosted by Field Marshal Bechtold in honor of Archduke Rainer, the Viceroy of the Lombard-Veneto Kingdom, to celebrate his return from his other capital of Milan to Venice. Andreas had to stifle a snarl of annoyance when he arrived to find Amelia already there and having her hand pawed by their attentive host.

"Your excellency!" Andreas said, struggling to stifle his desire to wrap his hands around the field marshal's beefy neck and squeeze it until his eyes popped from their sockets. "And Miss Coomb! I hope you remembered to save me a waltz."

"Of course," she said, smiling at him in relief.

It took him no time at all to extricate her from the field marshal's clutches.

"I must not have impressed upon you the importance of your leaving Venice at once," he said as they faced each other on the dance floor.

"You have, and I must say it would help tremendously if you would try to be a little *less* charming around my mother," she said tartly. "If she were ten years younger, she would pack me off to England posthaste and try to marry you herself."

"You alarm me, Miss Coomb," he said as he rested his hand lightly at the small of her back and took her dainty gloved hand in his. He had to smile in spite of himself.

"At the risk of feeding your outrageous vanity, you *must* know that your solicitude and your yellow roses have given birth to the most fanciful notions. She has been planning our marriage ever since. It was a great mistake to bring so many."

"Roses?" he asked. "But you may tell her that I had one of my servants pick them from my own greenhouse, so the gift was neither so personal nor so extravagant as it may have appeared."

"No doubt you find having your own greenhouse a great economy," she said sarcastically.

He laughed aloud but sobered instantly.

"My dear Miss Coomb, you *must* convince her."

"I am trying, I promise you," she said, looking apologetic. "Lady Madelyn is trying to help by pointing out how positively *haggard* I look at every opportunity, but that merely has served to convince my mother that Lady Madelyn only wishes to rid herself of a rival for your attention."

"Which she and I have deliberately suggested by our behavior so that we may conspire under cover of a flirtation," he said with a sigh of frustration. "Dear God, how I weary of all this pretending."

"I fear for you, Andreas," she whispered.

He suppressed the pleasure her words gave him.

"Save your fear for yourself," he said.

When the waltz came to an end, he led her to Lady Madelyn and her husband, whom he left with no choice but to partner Amelia while the count led Lady Madelyn onto the floor.

"You know, I have often regretted that I lost my mother so early in life," Lady Madelyn said ruefully when a movement of the dance brought them together, "but the sustained company of Mrs. Coomb makes me wonder if I should not thank the heavens instead. I sincerely pity our Amelia."

"I depend upon you to send them home to England at once," he said. "You must not fail."

"Do you think Amelia understands the significance of what she overheard?"

Andreas had to tell Lady Madelyn something of the truth to gain her cooperation in packing Amelia and her mother off to England, so he had told her merely that Amelia had blundered into a secret meeting between him and his compatriots on the day of the party at his villa. He knew Lady Madelyn would not question Amelia about what she had overheard because it would be awkward for her to reveal her own knowledge of the plot. Naturally Andreas did not tell Lady Madelyn that Amelia already knew that she was acting as an unofficial liaison between the conspirators and the British government. Nor did he tell her about Niccolò's original intention of assassinating the field marshal.

"She does. And it could be her death warrant."

Lady Madelyn looked searchingly into his face. He was the one to turn away.

"Andreas, you repeatedly have assured me that you can control these men, and I have relayed this assurance to Sir Gregory. I hope I do not need to tell you that should I have reason to doubt you can do as you say, I will be compelled to withdraw my support of your cause. I have a great regard for you, but my first loyalty is to my country."

There it was—the threat that would spell disaster for the struggle for his country's freedom.

"I can control them," he said.

"Then I fail to understand your urgency in sending Amelia home," she said with a dazzling smile to conceal the serious tone of their conversation. "If you truly control these men's actions, surely they would not take steps to silence Amelia without your knowledge and approval."

Was there ever such a dilemma?

Lady Madelyn must never suspect what a precarious hold he had on the firebrand who conspired to wrest the leadership of the conspiracy from him. Andreas did not doubt for a minute Niccolò would kill Amelia if he could. For the good of his cause and for her own safety, the girl must leave the country at once.

And he must tell Lady Madelyn any lie that would serve to enlist her aid in achieving this.

"You misunderstand. My sole fear is that Miss Coomb will reveal what she knows of our conspiracy in a thoughtless moment and her words will come to Austrian ears." He looked Lady Madelyn straight in the eye. "To prevent that, I would silence her myself."

Lady Madelyn's breath caught as his words sank in.

"My apologies," she said coldly. "I see that I have underestimated you."

He made her a slight, ironic bow of acknowledgment, and after that, her manner toward him was withdrawn.

Lady Madelyn now believed Andreas was ruthless enough to kill Amelia to protect the conspiracy. Of this he had no doubt. He had averted disaster for now, but it gave him no satisfaction.

"Signorina," whispered the masked man in the black domino who had entered through a door leading to the gardens.

He had been staring at Amelia for several moments while she waited in the elegant salon off the ballroom for Mr. Langtry to bring her the promised cup of punch. Her conversation with the count had so put her out of countenance that the kindhearted Mr. Langtry thought she was feeling faint.

Even as she told herself her sudden thrill of fear was foolish, she started to back away from the man clad in black. Mr. Langtry would return at any moment and, meanwhile, there were people all over the building. All she had to do was leave the room.

"Will you dance with me, signorina?" her asked in English, although his strong accent made the words barely intelligible.

It was *he*. That man who had wanted to kill her at Count Briccetti's villa. Now that he was no longer whispering, she recognized his voice.

"No, I thank you," she said, trying to keep her own voice steady. She knew instinctively that to betray her fear would be fatal. "My escort will be back in a moment."

She deliberately moved toward the center of the room, away from the doors that led to the garden.

"Such a pretty lady should not be alone," her tormentor said softly as he followed her. "I will keep you company until he returns."

"No," she said, backing toward the door that led to the hallway to the crowded ballroom. She was afraid to take her eyes off him. The man continued to stalk her with a faint, insinuating leer on his face. "Please, I do not want to dance," she cried out in panic.

A sharp intake of breath made her whirl around to look behind her. She had almost collided with a serving woman who was just entering the room.

"Forgive me, signorina," the serving woman said apologetically, even though it was Amelia who had not been watching where she was going. The woman's eyes narrowed as she looked into Amelia's face. "You are pale. Shall I inform your friends that you are ill?"

"I am well, I thank you," Amelia replied. Then she looked fearfully at her pursuer and saw his look of comprehension.

Horrified, Amelia realized that the serving woman had spoken in Italian, and Amelia had answered her in the same language.

"Will the signorina have a glass of wine to give her strength, then?" the serving woman persisted.

Amelia's throat was so dry with fright, she could hardly answer.

"You are very kind. Thank you," Amelia managed to say. The servant moved to a sideboard and poured ruby-colored liquid into a glass. To Amelia's relief, the dark man slipped silently from the room and back into the gardens.

She accepted the glass of wine from the servant.

The solicitous woman took her arm and guided her toward a sofa.

"You will feel better when the wine does its work," she said with a smile.

"You are very kind," Amelia repeated. Her hands were shaking when she took a sip. It was strong and surprisingly sweet. Then she remembered something she read in a novel from Minerva Press—red is the wine of choice for purposes of drugging and poisoning.

Her shaking hands lost their grip on the glass. It dropped to the floor in a crash that seemed loud to Amelia's heightened senses.

"Signorina!" exclaimed the servant. "You should sit down. You are ill."

Her concern seemed genuine, but Amelia could not take the chance that the servant was not the tool of the conspirator who sought to silence her. Had this woman and the man in the dark domino exchanged a significant glance before he made his escape? Amelia could not be sure.

"I am well, I promise you," Amelia said as she backed away from the servant. "I will go in search of my friends now."

She whirled and almost knocked over a lady just entering the room.

"I beg your pardon," she murmured as she ran away from the servant and the too-sweet wine.

The lights of the ballroom were ahead. Just before she reached them, a strong hand enclosed her arm in a viselike grip.

Amelia screamed.

"It is I, Miss Coomb," the count said as he chafed her chilled arms. Her skin was raised in gooseflesh.

"Oh, thank heaven," she said as she put her arm around his waist and pressed her face against his chest. He put his arms around her and laughed softly. She could feel his breath against her hair.

"It is all right," he murmured.

She stood back and looked up into his concerned eyes.

"That man is here. The one who wanted to kill me. It was horrible."

"I saw him. That is why I came in search of you." He smiled reassuringly at her. "Do not look so troubled, *carissima*. You are safe now."

"I know." She had almost stopped shaking. "I think one of the serving women tried to drug me—or poison me—with a glass of wine."

"My poor Amelia. Come with me. You will leave now."

He held out his hand, and she trustingly put hers into it.

"I will instruct my maid to pack as soon as I get back to the embassy," she told him as he conducted her out of the palace and onto the quay, where he signaled his gondolier to untie his gondola. "I will *make* my mother understand we must go home at once."

"I am afraid it is too late for that," he said as he assisted her into the boat.

"What do you mean?" she asked, puzzled when he stepped back onto the quay instead of joining her in the gondola. He made an imperious gesture with his hand to indicate the gondolier should depart.

Amelia let out a cry of horror when a man dressed in a black domino materialized beside her. In the darkness, she had not seen him crouching in the gondola. He wore the hood over his head so she could not see his face.

"Andreas!" she cried out in alarm as she scrambled out of the gondola. The count caught her in his arms to keep her from falling into the canal.

She looked back at the man in the gondola. Incredibly, he held out his arms for her and the count started to shove her back into the boat.

"Regrettably, my dear Amelia," the count told her, "you will not see the embassy again."

She tried to extricate herself, but he was too strong for her.

"Is there some problem?" called out an authoritative voice in Italian from another gondola.

"My lady friend has enjoyed a bit too much champagne," Andreas replied in the same language.

"My apologies, signore," said the other man, who obviously recognized the count.

Amelia started to cry out for help.

"Be silent," the count hissed as he covered her mouth with his hand. She bit into the flesh of his palm so hard, she tasted blood.

When he muttered an oath and snatched his hand away, Amelia filled her lungs with air and prepared to scream.

Before she could utter a sound, though, the count clipped her hard on the jaw and she felt the blackness close around her.

Andreas watched with regret as Amelia's face went slack and she sank into a pool of rich red-rose brocade. She looked like a crushed flower.

He lifted her limp body and handed her into the dark man's waiting arms.

"Take care that she is not seen," the count ordered with a gesture to the gondolier to leave.

The hooded man lowered the unconscious girl to the floor of the gondola, and the count shuddered with superstitious dread when he removed his domino and covered her with the black cloth to conceal her bright ball gown from sight.

Thirteen

Count Briccetti presented himself at the British Embassy at the unfashionable hour of nine o'clock the morning after the ball. The house seemed to be at sixes and sevens.

"Good morning, Andreas," Lady Madelyn said as she stood to welcome him.

"I came as soon as I received your note, my dear Lady Madelyn," he said with a slight bow. "In what way may I serve you?"

"Well, it is all a tempest in a teapot, as it turns out," she said with an embarrassed laugh. "My husband and I stayed late at the ball and Sir Gregory escorted Mrs. Coomb back to the embassy earlier in the evening. Robert and I thought, naturally, that Amelia had gone home with her mother. But Sir Gregory and Mrs. Coomb thought Amelia had stayed with us."

The count lifted one eyebrow in sardonic amusement.

"Ah, I begin to see. You thought that I had spirited Miss Coomb away in the night to have my wicked way with her."

"It was too bad of me," she admitted. "But it is all your fault for being so melodramatic." She lowered her voice in a skillful parody of his. 'To prevent that,' she intoned, 'I would silence her myself.' I was ready to believe you capable of any treachery."

Andreas laughed.

"Shall I assume, then, that Miss Coomb was found to be tucked up in her bed, safe and sound?"

"No, but apparently she went off with one of her friends on an excursion to Corfu. Her note arrived not ten minutes after I sent mine off to your house, explaining that she had gone home from the ball with Miss Lorimar's brother and sister-in-law and she would be grateful if her maid would deliver into the hands of the servant who bore the note her portmanteau, her boots, her cloak and several gowns since, presumably, she would feel quite conspicuous touring the Ionian Islands in a brocade ball gown and dancing slippers."

She gave a laugh with much relief in it.

"I shall speak quite sternly to her when I see her, I promise you," she added, "for frightening her mother and me half to death!"

"I am glad she is safe," he said, smiling at her. "When will she return?"

"In two weeks' time," Lady Madelyn said, lowering her voice, "which should effectively prevent her from disclosing any dangerous secrets. This does not materially alter our plans. Sir Gregory, my family, and I will depart for England in three days' time. Mrs. Coomb can hardly delay her return if Sir Gregory and I are determined to depart. Amelia will be quite bewildered to find us gone, but there is no help for it." She gave him a straight look. "I depend upon you to make sure that Amelia finds safe transportation to England when she returns from Corfu with Miss Lorimar."

Andreas bowed.

"It will be my very great pleasure."

"You will be informed when a decision is made with regard to the business matter we discussed," Lady Madelyn said.

"Thank you, dear lady," he replied, taking the hand she extended to him. "I will take my leave of you now. I am certain you have much to do before your departure."

"Farewell, Andreas," she said fondly as he brushed a fleeting kiss across her knuckles.

The smile faded from the count's face as soon as he was outside the cool walls of the embassy.

He signaled his gondolier and hardly saw the sun shining on the marble palaces that lined the Grand Canal, a view that usually never failed to delight him. When he arrived at Ca' Briccetti, he gave an absent nod at the liveried servant who opened the door for him, and made his way to the opulent bedroom that had been his mother's. He nodded at the burly servant who stood guard there and waited as he unlocked the door.

"How *could* you?" Amelia spat out when the count entered the room.

"I trust my servants have made you comfortable," he said blandly.

He gently traced with his finger the bruise that marred her beautiful skin.

"I am sorry for this," he said, appalled by the bluish mark. He had not meant to hit her so hard.

She slapped his hand away.

"My congratulations," he said. "Your note convinced them."

He had threatened an injury to her mother to persuade her to write it. Another stain on his honor.

"Am I to disappear, then?" she asked. Her voice

trembled. "Will you do it yourself, or will you turn me over to . . . them?"

He looked at her in astonishment, and the truth dawned on him.

She thought he was going to kill her.

"My poor Amelia. Did you think—you must know I would never harm you."

She touched the ugly bruise on her face as if to prove him false.

"There are iron bars on these windows. Very decorative, but iron bars just the same," she said, indicating the ornamental grille work. "I would not have told anyone what I overheard. I knew that to do so would endanger your life."

"I know that," he said, "but we are so close to success. Sir Gregory and Lady Madelyn will plead our case in London. Nothing must stand in our way."

"And that means *me,* I suppose." Her eyes were alive with indignation.

"Niccolò is not convinced that you will not give us away to our enemies, and I cannot watch you every minute. He *would* have killed you last night if I had not taken you away. Lady Madelyn, Sir Gregory, and your mother will sail for England on one of my ships in three days' time. At the proper moment, you will be taken aboard to join them."

He took her hands in his.

"You will be safe, I promise you," he said.

"And what about *you,* Andreas?" she asked. "Will you be safe?"

"I?"

"Listen to me," she said earnestly. "Those are evil men. They would slit your throat or mine without the slightest hesitation."

He gave a bitter laugh.

"Do you think I do not know it? But, unlike you,

I will give them no reason. Rest now, *carissima.* You have had a frightening experience, but all is well now."

She struck his conciliating hand away.

"How *dare* you patronize me!" she cried. "Quentin thought he was invincible too. Like you, he was caught up in some glorious cause. But he is dead just the same."

"And his people are free of the threat of Napoleon's yoke. Shall I do less to free my city from tyranny?" he asked. "Would you ask me to stop being a man?"

"Oh, you are a *man,* all right," she said in utter disgust.

A knock sounded at the door, and the count looked outside. Then he stepped back. A servant entered the room with Amelia's portmanteau.

"The ball gown is charming, but you may be more comfortable in these," he said. "I am afraid the servants had to remove your brushes, combs, and any other objects that might be used as weapons or tools to aid in your escape."

"How *very* thoughtful," she said, looking daggers at him.

"Not at all," he said mockingly. "The woman I send to wait on you will comb your hair and see to any other of your personal needs."

"You have thought of everything," she said, sounding testy. "One can tell you are quite experienced in entertaining women."

He bowed and started to leave.

"Andreas!"

He turned back.

"Take care," she whispered.

"It would have been better to slit her throat," Niccolò said contemptuously, "but the tenderhearted count must have his little plaything."

Andreas forced himself not to react to such blatant provocation. There was nothing his rival would have liked better than to draw him into a heated confrontation, and there were matters at stake more important than the disposition of one inconvenient Englishwoman. When six members of his conspiracy had appeared at the back door in the guise of deliverymen and asked to see him, he had received them in a secluded room of his palace and had his valet—whom he had cause to trust with his life—bring wine, bread, and cheese.

Niccolò swaggered over to the wine pitcher and poured himself a generous libation. It had been unavoidable, but Andreas made a dangerous enemy of him the day he slapped him down in front of the others for shooting Bassanio.

"I say it is time to show the Austrians that we are men, not sheep!"

"We will, when the British agree to stand beside us in the rebellion," Andreas said.

"Always the cautious one," Niccolò said. "It is a pity our leader grows faint at the sight of blood, like a woman."

"Take care, my friend," Andreas said softly, "or we shall see who grows faint at the sight of *your* blood."

He stood and advanced menacingly on Niccolò, who put down his wine and squared off with him.

"Peace, friends!" cried out one of the older men. "Remember that the *Austrians* are our enemies. We must not fight among ourselves, or we are lost."

Andreas let out the breath he had been holding.

Much as he would have enjoyed thrashing Niccolò, the man was right.

"I do not like being compared to a woman," Andreas said. "I give my men the right to speak freely in my presence, but my patience is not without limit."

Niccolò gave a careless wave of his hand, as if in apology.

"The woman is not important. She can live, for all I care."

"Gracious of you," Andreas said with a mocking smile.

"The field marshal has received an important commendation—he is to be honored at a grand parade and given a medal in the Piazza San Marco by the viceroy himself."

"You risked discovery for all of us by coming here to tell me that?" Andreas said with a shrug. "I knew this four days ago."

"The Austrians will know we are serious about throwing off their tyranny if the emperor's own brother, the viceroy, is killed right in the square surrounded by his soldiers."

"Then they can hunt us down like dogs and kill us one by one," Andreas said dampeningly. "Excellent plan."

Niccolò gave him a look of disdain.

"I suppose you would have us wait for your friends from England to come in with their troops to protect your back," he said. "And what would happen when the Austrians are driven out in your civilized little coup? Do you think your powerful friends will just turn and walk away?"

"We will draw up an agreement granting the English certain concessions," Andreas said just as if he had not explained all this before.

"Certain concessions," Niccolò scoffed. "The English will have the right to base ships in our harbor. Do you think they will be satisfied with that?"

"I have also agreed to provide certain objects from among my personal possessions. Those need not concern you."

"Pretty pictures," he said contemptuously. "When will you aristos learn? Did the Corsican bastard take the pretty pictures and the gold our leading citizens offered him and leave us to rule ourselves in peace? No! He stationed his soldiers in our city and squeezed us until we were dry. Are the Austrians satisfied to take from us the little that the French left behind? No! Do you think your good friends, the English, will take their army home after the battle is won? They will not! They will bleed us dry, like all the other foreign oppressors."

"Niccolò is right," one of the men said, moved by this passionate rhetoric.

"We need a man of the people to lead us!"

"Death to the viceroy!"

"No, no, my friends!" Andreas cried out. "If you kill the viceroy in a senseless act of violence, all will be lost. The Austrians will have the perfect excuse to tighten the yoke around our necks. And the British will never fight at our side, for they have a reputation as a civilized nation to protect. They will not give their support to a band of cutthroats who would assassinate the emperor's brother in cold blood, for that is how they would perceive us."

"I say there is nothing to choose between the Austrians and the British! We did not come here to ask your gracious permission, but to declare our intention."

Andreas looked at the other men's determined faces and knew he had been defeated.

"Are you with us or against us?" Niccolò asked in challenge.

"I cannot condone this killing," Andreas said.

"Then you must die," Niccolò said.

"No!" cried out another of the conspirators. "He is a friend of the Austrians, or so they think. To kill him before we kill the viceroy will put them on their guard."

"Then imprison him with his pretty English whore," Niccolò said. "You will stay here, count, and save your precious skin! We will watch you and intercept any messages you would send to warn our enemies. If you try to escape, we will kill you."

"Do not throw your lives away on a meaningless gesture!" Andreas cried. "Lady Madelyn and Sir Gregory will return to England soon to present our petition to their government. We must be patient a little longer."

"And once the British cast out the Austrians, who will you find to cast out the British?" another of the men replied. "Niccolò is right! Death to the viceroy!"

Andreas prepared to argue further, but Niccolò cut him off.

"Do not try my patience," he said with a sneer. "Or we shall find out if it is true you are more trouble dead than you are alive."

It was futile.

Andreas made a gesture of assent.

"So, *he* is your leader now," he said, indicating Niccolò. "Are you so eager to embrace martyrdom?"

"Now is the time to be men!" one of the other men declared.

"Take him away," Niccolò said with a gesture toward two of his companions. "Languish on your luxurious bed and eat sweetmeats. Amuse yourself with the English girl while I make a blow for freedom. If you behave yourself as our prisoner, we may decide to leave you alive."

Andreas contemptuously shook off the men when they grabbed his arms and pushed him toward the door.

"If you are wise, Count Briccetti," Niccolò said,

"you will give your servants no cause to suspect you are being compelled against your will, for we will kill any who offer us resistance. Two of us will be stationed here at all times. You are to instruct your servants to admit no one without our permission. Nor will any of them leave the house without our permission. Do you understand?"

"I understand," Andreas repeated.

His guards followed him out of the room and to the base of the twin staircases that led to the second floor.

They allowed him to proceed alone, but even when he was behind the walls of his bedchamber, he felt their eyes upon him.

Fourteen

"How fortunate that we will be here for the celebration," Lady Madelyn said to Mrs. Coomb in a vain effort to cheer that lady's spirits. "It should be a most impressive spectacle."

"I cannot think what possessed Amelia to go off to Corfu with Miss Lorimar without so much as a word to me!" Mrs. Coomb complained for at least the tenth time since breakfast. "You must believe Amelia the most ungrateful chit alive for taking herself off like that after you were kind enough to invite her to accompany you to Venice!"

"Not at all," Lady Madelyn said. "I brought her here to enjoy herself and recover from Lieutenant Lowell's death, and she seems to have done so."

"That is all very well," Mrs. Coomb said, "but she will not find an eligible husband touring the Ionian Islands with Miss Lorimar, I promise you. Miss Lorimar is a good enough girl, I suppose, but due to her circumstances, she hardly moves in the first circles, and you may depend upon it, the only men the girls are likely to meet are foreign persons of doubtful family. There is something about a foreigner that one cannot quite like, do you not agree?"

"As you say," Lady Madelyn said, forbearing to mention that Count Andreas Briccetti was a foreign person, and Mrs. Coomb had made it embarrassingly apparent that she would accept with pleasure an offer of marriage from him on Amelia's behalf.

"We have not seen Count Briccetti for some days," Mrs. Coomb said as if suddenly visited by happy inspiration. "Do you suppose he, too, was struck by a compulsion to tour the Ionian Islands?"

"Perhaps," Lady Madelyn murmured, willing to humor the lady, although she thought it doubtful. Indeed, she also was surprised that they had not seen more of the count. The preparations for the public celebration that would honor Field Marshal Bechtold as the defender of the kingdom were well under way, and she would have expected Andreas—in his role as Austrian friend and sycophant—to actively participate in the festivities leading up to it. He was quite a favorite with the viceroy, so Lady Madelyn had expected to see him at a party held the previous evening. He had failed to appear.

"Perhaps we might call on the count—with your husband's escort, of course," Mrs. Coomb suggested. Even she had to accept that it would be inappropriate for two ladies to call on a bachelor gentleman without a man to give their errand the aura of respectability. "He might be ill and in need of succor."

"His many servants may be trusted to take care of him in such a case," Lady Madelyn pointed out. "I am certain there is nothing amiss. One assumes his business interests require a great deal of his attention, and that, no doubt, accounts for his absence from society."

If Andreas thought it wise to distance himself from the British Embassy party, Lady Madelyn was certain he had good reason. Perhaps he had reason to think the Austrians suspected him of seeking to form an alliance with the British to overthrow Venice's military rulers. Lady Madelyn certainly was not going to permit Mrs. Coomb to barge into the count's palace and stir up trouble with her nosy questions.

She and Sir Gregory had kept the fact that they intended to return soon to England a secret from Mrs. Coomb and the embassy staff for fear the wrong persons would inquire too closely into the reasons for their departure. Lady Madelyn had been assured by the count that he would arrange for Miss Coomb's safe transportation home as soon as she returned from Corfu, and Madelyn had to be satisfied with that.

If a single hair on Amelia's head was harmed, she vowed, Count Andreas Briccetti would rue the day he was born!

Amelia's sudden decision to go to Corfu straight from the ball had seemed odd at first, but the decision made sense to Madelyn after she saw how Mrs. Coomb took on about it. Amelia's mother would naturally disapprove of any excursion that would take her daughter out of the enormously eligible Count Briccetti's orbit. Lady Madelyn had to admire the young lady's independence, but then, it was precisely what had attracted her to Amelia as a friend in the first place.

"Will you have another cup of tea, Mrs. Coomb?" she asked that disgruntled lady. "And another cake. They are quite delicious."

Mrs. Coomb accepted the tea, then turned eagerly toward the butler when he appeared at the door with a visiting card on his silver salver.

"Lady Madelyn, do you think the count . . . ?" she suggested coyly.

"Perhaps," she agreed with a smile as she nodded to the butler to present the card to her.

"It is Miss Lorimar," she said in puzzlement when she had read the card.

Mrs. Coomb clutched her heart.

"Has there been an accident?" she cried.

"Did the young lady seem distraught, Sheen?" Lady Madelyn asked her butler.

"No, my lady," the butler answered, wooden-faced. "Quite cheerful, if I may venture an opinion. She asked for Miss Coomb, my lady."

Madelyn was impressed despite her feeling of alarm. The butler did not betray the least curiosity about Miss Coomb's whereabouts. She knew she and Sir Gregory could depend upon Sheen's absolute discretion in the matter of his betters' affairs. It would not do, however, for the other servants to suspect that Miss Coomb was not where she should be.

Madelyn forced herself to be calm.

"Show Miss Lorimar in, if you please, Sheen," Lady Madelyn said as she patted the agitated Mrs. Coomb's hand. "We shall require some fresh tea. Bring it yourself, if you would be so good. And, Sheen, see that we are not disturbed while Miss Lorimar is here."

"Certainly, my lady," the butler said with a bow.

"Lady Madelyn, Mrs. Coomb," Miss Lorimar said when she was ushered into the room by the butler. "How kind of you to receive me at such an early hour." She looked about the room in pretty confusion, and her bright smile faded a bit in apparent disappointment. "Is Miss Coomb not yet arisen?"

"Miss Coomb is not here at present," Lady Madelyn said cautiously. She could feel Mrs. Coomb's agitation.

"Oh, I am sorry to hear it." Her surprise was unmistakable. "I hope she will not be gone long."

When the two ladies regarded her in silence, Miss Lorimar blushed crimson.

"What must you think of me, to barge in on you like this. By the happiest circumstance, my brother and sister-in-law decided to delay their departure from

Venice to Florence, and so I am free to go to Corfu with Miss Coomb after all. I came at once to tell Amelia the good news, and to see if it will suit her convenience to leave tomorrow. It is short notice, I know, but otherwise we will not be able to return before my brother's family goes on to Florence."

"What a pity," Lady Madelyn said, looking quite sternly at the alarmed Mrs. Coomb to command her silence. "Amelia will be gone for some time. It is a shame she did not know about your change of plan."

"How unfortunate," the disappointed girl said. She put on a brave smile. "If she should return sooner than expected, will you ask her to call on me? If she returns tomorrow or even the next day, I might still be free to go."

"I shall certainly do so," Lady Madelyn said, rising to indicate dismissal.

Miss Lorimar accepted it like a lady, to Madelyn's relief. She had to get rid of the girl before Mrs. Coomb recovered from her state of shock.

"Thank you," Miss Lorimar said, bowing to both ladies.

"I will see you out," Lady Madelyn said with a gracious smile. She did not want the girl to have the opportunity to ask any awkward questions of the servants. "I shall be right back," she added to Mrs. Coomb with a compelling look. "Wait for me here, if you please."

Mrs. Coomb merely nodded. Good. She was still too confused to speak, a state that Lady Madelyn was not optimistic enough to think would last for long.

Madelyn forced herself to walk Miss Lorimar to the door without apparent hurry, when what she wished to do was grab her arm and push her out the door with all haste.

To her relief, though, she found Mrs. Coomb still

in the parlor, devouring the sweet cakes, one after the other, in a sort of frenzy.

"What am I doing?" Mrs. Coomb cried out in agitation as she regarded the partially eaten cake halfway to her mouth as if it had been placed there by an unseen hand.

"I have often found indulging in sweets helpful to the exercise of rational cogitation," Lady Madelyn said as she helped herself to a chocolate eclair.

"Where can Amelia have gone?" Mrs. Coomb cried out.

Lady Madelyn swallowed the bite of creamy pastry in her mouth carefully as she sought an explanation that would not induce Mrs. Coomb to turn the household upside down at once.

Nothing came to mind.

Then, to her surprise, a look of elation came into the distraught mother's face. It was really quite bizarre.

"Do you suppose—oh, my dear Lady Madelyn, could they have eloped?"

"Eloped? What are you thinking of?" Madelyn asked, all at sea.

"Why, put two and two together and see what you get!" Mrs. Coomb said, clapping her hands in glee. "Amelia is missing . . . Count Briccetti is missing . . . do you see?"

Madelyn could only stare at her in astonishment.

"So you think Amelia and Count Briccetti have eloped?"

"Of course I do! Can you think of any other reasonable explanation?

Madelyn could, but she stifled the urge to say so.

Mrs. Coomb's interpretation of events would, at least, ensure her silence on the matter of Amelia's absence for the time being.

"Of course," Madelyn said slowly. "That would explain why she sent for her things in that mysterious way." She forced herself to giggle. "How naughty of Count Briccetti. I wonder that he could control his laughter at my expense when I told him about a messenger coming to fetch Amelia's belongings."

"How we will tease him when they return," Mrs. Coomb said, her eyes alight with triumph. "It is too wicked of Amelia to elope when she knows I have set my heart on a wedding at St. Paul's. Or perhaps in St. Mark's."

"You know how masterful Count Briccetti can be," Lady Madelyn said as she made a comical pantomime of fanning herself.

"Very true. Well, there is no help for it," Mrs. Coomb said, quite in charity with the world. "My dear son-in-law need not think he will have the last word in the matter. He has gotten his way for now, but when they return we shall plan a spectacular wedding, and so my girl may be married with all the consequence she deserves."

Mrs. Coomb gave Lady Madelyn a conspiratorial smile.

"My dear Lady Madelyn, I am certain I may rely on your discretion in this matter," she said. "It would not do for word of Amelia's absence to become known before the wedding announcement for fear of damage to her reputation."

"You may depend on me," said Lady Madelyn in relief.

"If you will excuse me, Lady Madelyn, I have many plans to make," Mrs. Coomb said as she wiped the crumbs from her fingers.

"Of course," Lady Madelyn said, smiling.

The smile faded as soon as the door closed behind Mrs. Coomb.

Where *was* Amelia?

She sent for one of her own servants who had accompanied her and her family from England, a man she valued for his discretion and absolute loyalty.

"Take this to Count Briccetti's palace," she said when he was admitted into her presence. She did not look up from her writing desk, where she was hastily penning an innocuous note desiring the count to join her family at the embassy for dinner that evening at eight o'clock. "And tell his servants that you were instructed to wait for a reply."

"Yes, my lady," the man said, receiving the note from her hands after she had sealed it with wax.

"And, Donald," she added. "Keep your eyes open. I would be interested in anything odd that you might observe while you are there. Try to see the count personally if you can contrive it."

The man bowed and was gone.

Fifteen

From behind the bars of her luxurious prison, Amelia could hear the revelers on the canal all night.

The field marshal's triumphant procession served as a perfect opportunity for Archduke Rainer, the viceroy of the Lombard-Veneto Kingdom, to cow the Venetian people with a show of military superiority and strength. For that reason, Amelia knew, all the Venetian citizens of any importance would be compelled to attend the celebration in addition to the common people.

Lady Madelyn, she imagined—even her own mother—would anticipate with pleasure the dancing in the square and the fireworks that evening, never realizing that Amelia was a prisoner in the count's palace a short distance away.

Amelia knew she might never see them again, for the mad, bloodthirsty men Count Briccetti had held so precariously in check finally had rebelled against their master. Ironically, he was now as much a prisoner as she.

Spectators were certain to be injured in the cross fire once the violence started. Would Amelia's mother and Mr. Langtry's innocent wards be among them?

"I am not hungry," she said without turning from the window when she heard the door open.

"It is a good thing," Andreas said solemnly, "for I bring no food."

Amelia turned around and looked at him.

His expression was grim, and he was dressed plainly in a buff-colored coat and breeches that appeared to have been borrowed from one of his servants. He wore a battered hat to conceal his fair curls.

"Where are you going?" she asked as a horrible suspicion dawned on her. "Never mind," she cut in angrily when he would have spoken. "You are going to try to get past your guards and out onto the square to prevent the assassination. Of course. And in the process, you will be killed."

"If I do not, the viceroy will be killed and Austria will inflict terrible suffering on my people in retaliation. I must stop this if I can, no matter what the risk."

"Why does every man I care for have to be so *noble?*" Amelia sniffed.

Andreas gave her a wintry smile.

"One can only admire your excellent taste," he said. "Listen, my dear, I have arranged with some of my loyal servants for your escape as well. Once you are away from the palace, no one will notice you and my servant in the streets with so many people in them. If I am captured or killed, you must not be found here, or you will be implicated in the plot."

He took her hands.

"I never meant to lead you into danger."

She released a pent-up breath.

"I know," she said. "You mean to bring it only upon yourself!"

"One of my ships is waiting at harbor, ready to embark for England. My servant will escort you there. It will sail as soon as you are on board."

She stared at him in disbelief.

"Do not look so surprised. I am an old hand at plotting intrigue. Farewell, Amelia," he said as he kissed her on the forehead. "I hope you will find happiness someday."

With a cry of distress, Amelia threw her arms around his neck and felt his arms go around her.

"I have been trying so hard to be good," he said wryly as he pressed his lips to hers.

The kiss was long and lingering. It had all her heart in it.

"You have had some practice in the years of our separation," he whispered when they finally had to break apart to breathe.

"Don't," she snapped as she pushed her hands against his chest to free herself. He held her tightly.

"I apologize," he said ruefully. "When one is at a loss for words, one too often comes up with the wrong ones." He gave her a wry smile. "I do not deserve it, but may I hold you a little longer?·It may be for the last time."

"You horrid man," she said with a breaking voice as she rested her head against his shoulder.

"Yes, I know," he said as he stroked her hair. He kissed her cheek as if in apology. She could feel him trembling.

"Andreas?" she said questioningly.

He tried to smile.

"I am not quite so brave as you seem to think," he admitted. "I have never set out to stalk and kill a man, certainly not a man I know as well as I know Niccolò. I am not sure I can do it."

"Come with me, then," she cried out. "Let us get on your ship together and sail away."

"It is cruel of you to tempt me, *carissima.* I cannot. I am responsible for these men because I was their leader. It is *I* who have nurtured their dreams of freedom and placed them on this destructive path. I will not run away now to save myself while they bring the Austrians' wrath upon my people."

He framed her face with his hands and looked deeply into her eyes.

"I ask you, Amelia, could you respect a man who would do such a thing?"

He placed his fingers over her lips.

"Do not bother to give me the lie, for I know you could not."

"Andreas—"

"Be safe, Amelia," he said.

He gave her a brief, hard kiss and left the room.

The diversion his valet had designed worked perfectly, and Andreas was able to escape from one of the windows and lower himself from a rope to the ground while his former co-conspirators rushed to see what had made the resounding crash on the other side of the palace. Upon investigation, they were to find a bookcase broken under the seeming weight of some priceless leather-bound volumes. And if they thought to check on the count himself, they would find a servant of about the count's physical size, tucked into the count's bed with his back to the door, wearing his master's most ornate nightshirt and an embroidered bed cap to conceal his head. It was this servant's clothes Andreas borrowed for his escape.

During the days of his captivity, Andreas had made it a point to retire to his room for a nap in the same nightshirt and cap at the same time each afternoon, so his guards were accustomed to see the lump of his body under the covers and the tasseled cap protruding at the top.

It was a simple matter for the count to blend in with

the many citizens walking to the Piazza San Marco for the celebration. He hoped Amelia and the servant he trusted to escort her to his ship would enjoy the same luck in escaping that Andreas had. Fortunately, most of his former co-conspirators would be at the piazza to incite the populace to rise against the Austrians after, presumably, the viceroy's assassination would leave them in disarray.

The piazza was, as Andreas expected, crowded with citizens. He could see the Austrian soldiers lining the newly erected platform upon which the ceremony would take place, but they looked far from alert in their dress uniforms.

They were not expecting trouble from the subjugated masses.

Andreas moved through the crowds with his hat moved forward to shadow his face, as if from the sun. It would not do for him to be recognized.

With luck, he could find Niccolò and immobilize him without a shot fired. If *he* were going to attempt to assassinate the viceroy, he would do so from the vantage point of the basilica itself.

He approached the basilica and searched the façade. A glint of metal betrayed by the sunlight revealed the assassin's hiding place within the shadow of one of the archways. Andreas, abandoning all pretense of stealth, broke into a run.

Amelia was ready when the count's servant came to collect her.

She had washed her face with cold water to hide the evidence of her weeping and donned her plainest gown with her cloak fastened at the neck and the hood covering her head. She hoped she made a convincing servant girl. By fortunate coincidence, the count happened to employ a servant of Amelia's own size and coloring. The girl would stay out of sight while Amelia sought to escape by impersonating her.

Amelia *had* to be convincing. The count's former compatriots would think nothing of murdering her if they caught her trying to escape.

The servant allowed her to precede him out the doorway of her prison. He was one of the count's burlier footmen, although today he wore no livery. His clothes were respectable, though a trifle shabby, and Amelia had the impression they were his own.

Amelia stole a glance at the man and wondered if he knew where his master had gone.

To Amelia's dismay, he put an arm around her and drew her close to his side when they had walked down the back stairs and were about to go out the door to freedom.

"Your pardon, signorina," he whispered, indicating with a jerk of his head the men who lounged at some distance from the doorway watching who went in and out. "They are to think we are servants on the holiday, yes?"

"Yes," Amelia replied softly as she turned her face from the watching men. Her companion brushed his lips across her forehead.

"Where are you going?" challenged one of the men when he had swaggered up to them.

"To see the viceroy and find a cozy place for our own celebration, eh, *cara?*" the servant said with a leer.

The questioner reached for Amelia's hood to look at her face, but she batted his hands away.

"Let go of me, you pig!" she spat out at him in Italian and clutched the servant's hand.

The servant gave a convincing laugh.

"My Deloria does not wish any to see her face, for

she is married to a jealous man, do you understand? He would beat her if he knew she left the house with me."

The man's eyes narrowed, but his companion waved them away with a show of impatience.

Amelia's escort gave her a smile of approval as they proceeded from the palace.

"It is a pity we must miss the ceremony," she said in Italian.

"I speak the English well enough, signorina," he whispered with a touch of injured pride. "We must go in the direction of the piazza if we are to put their suspicions at rest. Once there, we can make our way to the ship."

Amelia nodded in agreement; nothing could please her more.

The piazza was precisely where she wished to be.

They blended in with the crowd of people approaching the festivities and found the Piazza San Marco rimmed with vendors and their colorful wares. She insisted upon buying a peach from one of them and offered a bite to her companion.

A fanfare burst from a brace of trumpets; the viceroy, riding a white horse, entered the square with the field marshal at his side, also on horseback. A procession of cavalry officers formed their honor guard.

"We must go now, while they are all looking at the viceroy," the servant whispered as he bent to sink his teeth into the peach. "The master will want us away before the trouble starts."

Amelia smashed the ripe fruit into his startled face and ran behind the vendor's stall to hide from him.

Andreas threw himself upon the startled assassin just as he fired, sending the bullet into the stone archway. It ricocheted off the building and back toward the struggling men.

The count staggered when it slammed into his body.

"Run, fool! Save yourself," he said to Niccolò, but he saw the idiot was determined to stand his ground. The ferver of a fanatic shone in Niccolò's eyes as, incredibly, he fumbled to reload. By then, booted feet were pounding the stones of the square toward them as the crowd fell back. When he saw it was hopeless, Niccolò bared his teeth and swung his weapon like a club toward the approaching soldiers.

Andreas ran into a cluster of screaming people as the soldiers converged upon Niccolò and wrested his weapon from him.

Stupid. Andreas should have killed Niccolò himself instead of leaving him alive to be captured by the Austrians. The small handgun he had concealed on his person would serve the purpose at such close range.

Now the Austrians would torture the names of all the conspirators out of Niccolò. Andreas found at the crucial moment that he was incapable of taking the life of the nephew Father Dominic had loved as a son, even though his decision would mean death for all of them.

"Death to the oppressors!" the foolhardy Niccolò called out.

Andreas flinched at the sickening sound of fists striking flesh behind him. As he ran through the square, using the confusion of the crowd as a shield, he could feel the sticky blood flow against his thigh. The wound burned as if his flesh were on fire.

"Are you all right, signore?" asked a man when he staggered.

"He is drunk. We will take care of him," a feminine voice said.

"You?" Andreas said wonderingly as Amelia slipped

under his arm on his uninjured side to support him. His servant took his other arm.

"Can you make it to the palace, master?" the servant asked.

"Yes," Andreas said, gritting his teeth.

"Amelia, what are you doing here?" He gave his servant an accusing look. "I ordered you to take her to safety!"

"Save your strength," Amelia hissed, "and keep your voice down. Did you think I would abandon you?"

"You should not have endangered yourself."

"Don't like it, do you?" she asked smugly. Her voice grew dim in the ringing of his ears. "We're losing him," she told the servant. "Don't let him fall!"

Amelia stood looking out the window of the count's bedchamber while the valet finished undressing his barely conscious master. It had not surprised her to find upon their return from the piazza that all of Andreas's co-conspirators who had been guarding the palace the past few days had fled like rats from a sinking ship.

"You should not be here," Andreas croaked from the bed behind her. She turned to face him.

The valet bowed to Amelia in passing as he left the room. The count was now dressed in a fine white linen nightshirt with his hair brushed to a high gloss. The valet had also cleaned and dressed his wound, for the bullet had passed straight through the count's thigh without encountering muscle or bone.

It did not seem odd to her in the least that the count's valet was so skilled at dressing bullet wounds.

"I will leave you to rest," Amelia said to the count.

"No," he said as he struggled to sit up on his elbows. The expression of pain that crossed his face had Amelia running in alarm to press him back down on the bed.

"You will tear it open again," she told him. "You must lie still."

"It is of no importance," he said. "You must leave at once for the British Embassy. Do you not understand that the Austrians will come for me now? They will question Niccolò under torture; they will have the names of all the conspirators soon if they do not have them already. Go now. No one will stop you."

"And leave you to face them alone? Be still," she said. "I will send for Lady Madelyn. She will know what to do."

"She is in no position to—"

A hard knocking on the outside door below caused Amelia to put her hand to his lips. They stared at each other as heavy footsteps echoed on the marble floor below.

"Take off that nightshirt," Amelia commanded as she tore at the laces of her gown.

"What are you doing?" Andreas asked in astonishment as she emerged from the gown in her lacy chemise. Then understanding apparently dawned, and to Amelia's relief he started pulling the nightshirt over his head. Amelia had to help him, and even at that he was gasping by the time he was freed of it.

"I should probably take this off too," she said self-consciously as she looked down at her virginal white chemise, "but—"

At that moment a heavy knocking sounded on the bedchamber door.

"Signore," said the count's steward as he burst into the room. His upper lip was dotted in sweat. "There are soldiers here. They wish to question you."

"Admit them," said Amelia, blushing, as she got

into the bed with Andreas and put her bare arms around his bare shoulders.

"I cannot permit you to—" the count began.

She stopped his words with a kiss as the soldiers shoved the steward aside and stamped into the room.

Andreas broke off the kiss and exchanged a look of comprehension with Amelia.

Then he managed to summon up a little of his old arrogance.

"What is the meaning of this intrusion?" he demanded with brows knitted together.

Even so, his face was pale and he could not quite conceal the shaking of his limbs. Amelia saw the look of contemptuous amusement that crossed the soldiers' faces.

There was a flurry of activity outside, and the field marshal strode into the chamber. He was still dressed in his ceremonial uniform.

"Excellency," Andreas said weakly. "You honor my house. I would stand to greet you properly, but you have caught me at a disadvantage."

"You were expected to attend the ceremony today, Count Briccetti," the field marshal said with a menacing look at Andreas. He spoke English, presumably in deference to Amelia. "It was a command, not a request."

"I beg your forgiveness," Andreas said. He gazed into Amelia's eyes and caressed her shoulder. "I was . . . detained."

The field marshal gave a short laugh.

"On a matter of grave importance, I perceive," he said with a leer at Amelia. "Your absence *was* somewhat suspicious. An assassin attempted to kill the viceroy, but by the grace of God he failed. He is in our custody, although his wounded accomplice escaped. Under questioning this villain, who calls himself Niccolò Soranzo, has denounced you as his accomplice in a conspiracy to overthrow Austrian rule. What have you to say to that?"

"I?" Andreas asked, sweating heavily now.

"I have been with the count all day," Amelia declared. The field marshal turned in her direction, and she felt her face flame at the lascivious look he gave her. "And for the past several nights," she added.

"Please, my dear," the count said, placing his hand over hers. "I will answer for myself." He faced the field marshal. "On my word of honor, I did not plot the viceroy's death. Can you accuse me of such a thing after I have entertained him at my own table?"

His voice rang of conviction. His words were true after all.

"And you do not know him, this Niccolò Soranzo?" Andreas hesitated.

"He is the nephew of my former tutor, Father Dominic Soranzo. I had a kindness for the boy when he was young, but we have been estranged for some time. He must have denounced me from spite."

"Father Dominic Soranzo, the troublemaking priest," the field marshal said slowly. "Yes, it fits. Under ordinary circumstances I would insist upon having my men examine your body for the wound——"

The way he looked at Amelia made her cringe against the cushions. She gave a faint cry of alarm that was not at all feigned as she pulled the linens up high and drew closer to Andreas. He put a protective arm around her, but it was visibly trembling. The Austrians would naturally assume it was from cowardice.

The field marshal laughed.

"I think we will spare the lady further distress," he said with a gallant bow toward Amelia. He nodded dismissal to the soldiers, who obediently filed from the room. "I must admit I found it hard to envision you in the role of reckless conspirator," the field marshal added to Andreas with a smile of contempt, "after our generosity to you."

"A word with you, excellency," Andreas said when he would have left as well.

"Yes?"

"My . . . companion," he said, indicating Amelia. "Her friends at the British Embassy and her mother believe she has gone with a female friend on a tour of the Ionian Islands. If they discover otherwise, it would be quite awkward for her, and damaging to her reputation."

"It shall be our secret," he said, amused. "I must say, Miss Coomb, you surprise me. I will look forward to our further acquaintance."

His slow perusal of her figure inadequately concealed by the thin bed linens made her want to sink with humiliation.

"Carry on, my friends," the field marshal said genially, and turned to leave.

"You do know you will be the talk of the taverns by evening," the count said when they were alone again.

"I know," she said. She could not keep her lower lip from trembling. "My poor mother."

"I will make this right by you, *carissima,*" he said. "I swear it."

Andreas sat up and lowered his legs over the side of the bed but had the presence of mind to pull the linens over to pool in his lap in order to protect his modesty. The poor girl's innocence had been compromised enough for one day.

"What are you doing?" Amelia cried.

"I must call on your mother before—" He broke off and cradled his head in both hands.

"Andreas, you must lie still," he heard her say in

alarm as she eased him back against the pillows. His vision darkened and he clutched her hand, willing himself to remain conscious.

A curious ringing filled his ears, and then he heard nothing.

Sixteen

"Amelia?" the count said drowsily. Suddenly his eyes flew open and he sat straight up in bed. "Amelia!"

"I am here," Amelia said as she rose from the chair beside the bed and touched his brow with cool fingers.

"You should not be," he said. "Your reputation—"

"My reputation was lost the moment we were discovered together. Lie still. You are far from well."

It had been two days since the field marshal barged into the count's chamber and gallantly declined to search the count for bullet holes because of Amelia's presence in his bed.

The count's raging fever had broken in the night, but it left him weak and muddled in his thinking. His nightshirt and bed linens were saturated in sweat. His hair was damp.

Amelia touched his cheek, but he turned away from her.

It was humiliating to appear like this before the woman who had sacrificed so much for him. She had been confined for days in his house, and what had he done for her entertainment? Bled copiously all over her and vomited in the chamber pot she held for him.

He had begged her to let his valet care for him, but she had insisted upon sharing the responsibility with him of nursing Andreas back to health.

"I must get dressed," he said. "The world will accept that I have spent two days in seclusion with my *chère amie,* but I must show myself in the city now or invite the Austrians' suspicions that all is not as it should be."

"It is too soon," she protested.

She could not have been more tender if he were a child, but Andreas did not want her comfort now. He did not deserve it.

He did not deserve *her!*

Andreas had failed his country and, to make matters worse, he had hidden behind a woman's skirts to elude his enemies. How could he not be less than a man in her eyes?

His former co-conspirators, he knew, were scattered, imprisoned, or dead already, for Niccolò must have broken under torture and denounced them by now.

The Austrians would make a bloody example of them to affirm their power.

But Count Briccetti, the oppressors' friend and sycophant, would continue throwing parties in their honor, flirting respectfully with their wives and daughters, and paying them exorbitant bribes so that his ships could continue to sail the seas and add to his coffers unimpeded.

His position as the Austrians' lapdog had been degrading enough when he could believe that soon he would vindicate himself in the eyes of those who thought him a coward and traitor to Venice.

Now it was unspeakably humiliating. He looked ahead to the future and saw despair.

"I am well enough," he said more harshly than he intended. "You will not keep me prisoner in my own house."

Looking hurt, Amelia stood back.

"Miss Coomb," he said, reaching for her hand. "Forgive me."

"Of course, you are right," she said as she evaded his hand and walked to the door. "I will call your valet to dress you now."

"Amelia!" he called out when she closed the door behind her. The door opened a moment later, but it was his valet who stepped inside the room.

"I need a bath, breakfast, a shave, and clothes," the count snapped at his faithful servant. He gave the valet a glare that forbade him to argue.

When he looked like a man again, he would make his peace with Amelia.

Amelia heard heavy booted steps on the marble stairway to the upper floor, and the hair stood up on the back of her neck.

"The Austrians," she breathed, terrified that Andreas's part in the aborted uprising had been discovered and they were coming to kill him after all.

But the voice that floated up the staircase was not that of a soldier.

"Stand aside at once! I *will* see the count!"

"Mother," Amelia gasped as she ran to the banister of the gallery and looked upon the spectacle of her mother defiantly staring up at the burliest of the count's footmen on the step above her. At her back were Lady Madelyn and her husband.

"Amelia!" Mrs. Coomb cried out when she saw her daughter. "My poor darling! What has that fiend done to you?"

Amelia ran down the stairs to her mother.

"Mother, you don't understand—" she said.

Mrs. Coomb gave a harsh laugh.

"Oh, I *understand*," she said bitterly. "I understand

that Count Briccetti has ruined my innocent child! Where *is* he? Where is the vile seducer?" She raised her voice so it rang against the marble walls. "Count Briccetti! Show yourself!"

"Mother, *no!*" Amelia said. "You must not—"

"Hush, daughter. I will take care of you now," she said as she enfolded Amelia in her arms. She raised her head. "*There* you are, you villain!"

Amelia swiftly turned around and saw the count standing at the gallery railing.

He wore a meticulously tailored coat in blue super-fine. Not a single crease marred the perfection of his buff pantaloons, and Amelia fancied one could see one's face in the gloss of his boots.

He was nothing less than imperial as he strode down the steps to join them.

To her mother, Lady Madelyn, and Mr. Langtry he no doubt appeared the very image of the bored, languid aristocrat. But to Amelia's more knowledgeable eyes, he looked as if he might fall over if one breathed too hard in his direction.

"Mrs. Coomb, I implore you," he said with a faint, ingratiating smile. "Let us step into the salon and discuss the matter." He turned to the footman. "Refreshments for my guests," he commanded.

"Do not come over the lord with me," snarled Mrs. Coomb. "You have ruined my daughter, and you will answer for it. No respectable man will have her now, and you *will* make an honest woman of her, or I shall proclaim your perfidy throughout the city!"

"Mother, please," whispered Amelia, and, to her humiliation, burst into tears of reaction.

"Hush, Amelia," her mother said, patting her shoulder. "He shall pay for what he has done to you."

"Mother, I beg of you—"

"Listen to her, Count Briccetti," Mrs. Coomb said

reproachfully. "Still she defends you, even though you have abused her shamefully. All the gossips in Venice are laughing behind their hands at us. Amelia's name is being bandied about in every taproom in the city."

"Mrs. Coomb," Count Briccetti said slowly. Amelia could see the effort it was taking for him to remain upright. "Let us talk this over like civilized—"

"I am taking my daughter home, sir," Mrs. Coomb said defiantly. "You have not heard the last of this."

"I implore you, madam—"

Amelia took one of his hands and pressed it. He turned his eyes to her, and she could see that they were slightly unfocused.

"I will go with my mother," she told him. When he opened his lips to object, she touched them with the tips of her fingers. "It is best."

"Amelia," the count said. He grasped her hand when she would have withdrawn it.

"Let go of my daughter!" Mrs. Coomb shrieked. "Have you not done enough?"

"I am ready to leave with you, Mother," Amelia said. Her eyes did not leave the count's. "Please take me away from here."

"Of course, my love," Mrs. Coomb said at once. She threw her head back and glared at the count. "You have not heard the end of this, Count Briccetti!"

Black dots danced across his eyes, but Andreas could clearly see the distress on Amelia's face as her mother swept her from the room.

When he would have followed the women, Mr. Langtry caught his arm in a grip painful enough to clear his head a little.

"Let it rest," Mr. Langtry said in a menacing voice.

"Get your hands off me," the count snarled. He was appalled at how weak his words sounded.

"*Think*, Andreas," Lady Madelyn said, giving her

husband an approving nod when he increased his grip on Andreas's arm to keep him from extricating himself. "It is natural for a mother to fly to the defense of a daughter who has been wronged. We tried to keep the gossip from her ears, but we could not do so forever. It was inevitable that she should learn what was being said about you and Amelia."

"I cannot let her leave me like this—"

"It appears to me as if she's already done it," Mr. Langtry said. The contempt in his voice made Andreas wish he had the strength to strike him.

If he tried now, he would be lucky not to fall on his face.

"Robert, darling," Lady Madelyn said. "Will you not go outside with Mrs. Coomb and Miss Coomb? I shall join you in a moment."

It sounded more like a command than a request.

"As you wish, my dear," Mr. Langtry said as he released Andreas. Then he went out the door with a last look of disgust in Andreas's direction.

"How much does he know?" Andreas asked Lady Madelyn when they were alone.

"I have not discussed the nature of our previous conversations with him, if that is what you are asking," she said, raising one eyebrow. "He knows only that we have come here to rescue Miss Coomb from further disgrace at your hands. But my husband is not stupid. He suspects some deeper intrigue. And, Andreas," she added significantly, "the Austrians are not stupid either."

Andreas gave her a sharp look. She had his full attention now.

"The Austrians," Lady Madelyn continued, lowering her voice, "are watching your house. Today they have seen something that corroborates your story that you have been amusing yourself the past several days with your *chère amie* rather than, say, recovering from a bullet wound sustained during a failed assassination attempt."

His mouth fell open.

"How did you know?"

"Did you think Sir Gregory would not have spies of his own? The man who shot at the viceroy. He was one of yours, was he not?" Her voice was as hard as flint.

Andreas gave a long sigh. Why bother to deny it?

"Yes. But he acted without my order."

"So much for your claim that you could control your group of revolutionaries."

He could only stare stupidly at her. Why must his head be full of cotton wool when he needed it to be clear?

"I would further suppose," she went on, "that the reason you did not break my husband's jaw is because you could not win a fight with a kitten in your present condition."

He made her an ironic bow and was instantly sorry for it. It made his head spin.

"All is not lost, however," she said. "You can still save yourself. The Austrians are eager to represent the incident as the act of a single crazed fanatic. They pride themselves on the fiction that they are an enlightened power. They would not want to acknowledge that the attempted coup had the backing of a certain Venetian aristocrat prominent in international society, for then it would have to be taken seriously. And they would look foolish for having admitted you into the circle of their intimates."

She gave him a smile that was not without sympathy.

"Your heroic action in stopping the bullet meant for the viceroy has done much to redeem you in my eyes and in Sir Gregory's," she assured him. "Unfortunately, although we hold you in considerable esteem personally, we regret that we cannot recommend that Britain support you in your effort to free Venice from Austrian rule at this time. This assassination attempt against the emperor's brother changes everything. Britain cannot afford the perception that she is willing to encourage a mere band of anarchists to revolt against their rightful masters."

"I know it," he said with a heavy sigh.

"It is fortunate for you," Lady Madelyn said with an edge to her voice, "that Amelia was available to distract the field marshal from your infirmities. She was here all the time, was she not?"

"Yes," he admitted, shamefaced. He should have known better than to try to conceal anything from this woman. She had ingested a talent for intrigue with her mother's milk.

"Miss Lorimar called on us, you see, and innocently put paid to your clever invention of the excursion to Corfu," she told him. "Fortunately, one of my servants contrived to get one of your off-duty footmen drunk and find out about the young Englishwoman who was your guest, and that the servants were to keep her presence secret. Otherwise, you may believe I would have turned the entire city upside down to find her. I had hoped to keep the business quiet in order to preserve her reputation. But no one in Venice believes Amelia is a virgin now—not after living unchaperoned in your house for several days. Especially not after the field marshal and a handful of his soldiers discovered her with you in your bed."

"I swear to you on the graves of my parents that the girl is untouched."

Lady Madelyn's face softened.

"I know that," Lady Madelyn said as she reached

out to touch his hand. "You are incapable of acting with such dishonor. But if you wish to remain alive, you will keep the Austrians ignorant of this fact."

"In other words, I must continue to hide behind Miss Coomb's skirts."

"Only if you wish to remain alive," she said dryly. "It is a pity that Amelia's reputation has suffered, but there is nothing you can do about that now. The damage is done."

"I must go after her—I must explain," But Andreas's head reeled dizzily, and he was forced to accept Lady Madelyn's support to a chair.

"Andreas, you *must* not show yourself abroad in this state!" she warned him. "The Austrians must not suspect you were wounded! Will you let Amelia's sacrifice have been for nothing?"

Andreas took a deep, steadying breath and cursed his infirmity.

She was right.

There was nothing he could do for Amelia now. Not until he was whole again.

Amelia unwrapped the white box of yellow roses and nodded to her maid to take them away and put them in water.

Her bedroom was filled with the count's fragrant offerings—he had sent a bouquet every day since she was dragged from his palace in disgrace.

She knew he meant it in kindness and possibly in apology.

But not one of these ostentatious floral tributes was accompanied by a personal note—just his visiting card and a scrawled signature.

"Why does he not come?" Mrs. Coomb said petulantly when she saw the count's latest offering.

Amelia could think of only one reason.

He did not care for her after all. He was a nobleman who could have his choice of beautiful, aristocratic women.

Why should he settle for Amelia merely because she had deliberately compromised her reputation in order to save his life?

At first Amelia was worried sick that the fever had come back, but Lady Madelyn casually reported seeing him at a party.

Since then he had been seen all about the city.

Neither Mrs. Coomb nor Amelia, of course, had gone out in public since they had returned from Count Briccetti's palace on that fateful day. It would be too humiliating to hear the whispers all around them. No one who was anyone would have deigned to acknowledge them anyway.

There had been no more parties hosted by the British Embassy. No doubt Sir Gregory and Lady Madelyn were embarrassed by her presence, although both were too polite to say so.

Amelia saw the count only once, at a distance from her balcony as he rode in his gondola down the Grand Canal toward the Doges' Palace. He had been dressed formally in black, and no doubt he, like Lady Madelyn and Sir Gregory—and unlike Amelia and her mother— had been invited to the official reception to welcome the Belgian ambassador to Venice.

It was clear that *he* was not ostracized by society.

The count had looked up toward her window, but she stepped back out of sight to avoid his gaze.

She would *not* be caught mooning after him like a lovesick idiot.

The following day there was no floral tribute. Nor on the next.

The day after that, Lady Madelyn mentioned in

passing that Count Briccetti had set sail in his flagship for some undisclosed destination.

"The evil man," Mrs. Coomb fumed. "Do not fret, Amelia. The villain will do right by you, or he will answer to me! Even if I must go after him myself and drag him back to Venice to do his duty!"

Amelia gave a despairing sigh.

Her poor mother.

Mrs. Coomb had come to Venice to enjoy herself. Instead, she was forced to hide away from society, ashamed to show her face in public.

As for the count, he had left the city to avoid her.

Amelia was an embarrassment to him, no doubt, like she was to her mother, Lady Madelyn, Sir Gregory, and the entire British delegation.

She owed it to all of them to disappear.

That afternoon while her mother was napping, Amelia stole out of the house with her portmanteau and pulled her cloak around her face.

With luck she would be aboard ship by the time her mother and Lady Madelyn found her letter, and it would be too late for them to stop her.

Indeed, she could think of no reason why they would want to.

Seventeen

A profitable week at sea restored Andreas's health better than any physic could have. When his fever recurred, he had been left with no choice but to have his servants and his physician spirit him away from Venice and the suspicious eyes of the Austrians. There was no way he could continue to appear in public without revealing his infirmity.

It had been good to blend into the masculine rhythm of shipboard life.

It had been good to have time to think.

Now that he was once again a whole man, he would make things right between himself and Amelia.

Dressed with unusual care even for him in his most opulent clothes, Andreas disembarked from his gondola and sauntered up to the door of the British Embassy with several footmen carrying selected tokens of his esteem in his wake.

The gossips who considered the woman he loved damaged goods would be silenced when she was seen abroad in the long rope of lustrous pearls now resting in the gold coffer he would present as his engagement gift. They would be overcome with admiration when she glowed with pride in a gown made of the gold-shot cerulean silk he had placed in the hand-carved sandalwood chest with his own hands.

It would have been demeaning to her pride and his for them to have married in haste, as if their union were something shameful, to be hidden.

His lovely Amelia deserved to be a bride with all the attendant pomp of marriage to a noble of Venice. He would show the world how much he valued her.

Andreas might have failed his country, but he would *not* fail her.

With a flourish, he handed his gilt-edged card to the butler at the embassy and asked to see Mrs. Coomb.

"Proud as a cockerel on your own dunghill, aren't you, old chap?" remarked Mr. Langtry when the count and his entourage were ushered into a plain green parlor, the one used for receiving tradesmen and other persons of merely respectable rank.

Andreas frowned. He had always been shown to the gold salon before, the one reserved for important visitors of state. He had never seen this particular room, but he knew it at once for what it was.

"Is Mrs. Coomb not here?" A horrible thought struck him. "She and her daughter have not returned to England?"

"No, nothing like that," Mr. Langtry said. "But I will leave Mrs. Coomb to tell you the details. She will be with you in a few moments." He glanced over the gold casket and the sandalwood chest with raised eyebrows. "I am afraid this is going to be a case of too much too late."

Too late?

Before Andreas could demand to know what he meant by that, Mrs. Coomb flew into the room and faced him with a ferocity he remembered all too well. She stopped dead in her tracks when she saw the rich gifts and the liveried servants.

"What is all this?" she asked.

"Gifts for my future bride, if she will have me," Andreas said, although he was in little doubt of the outcome, really.

"Oh, so you have come to buy her good name back for her, have you?" she scoffed. "It is about time!"

"May I have your daughter's hand in marriage?" he asked with his most charming smile, the one that melted ambitious mothers' hearts like so much wax.

"You will have to ask *her,*" she snapped. "She has said she will not have you even though I have done my best to impress upon her that her only choice is to marry you or face ruin."

Andreas's confidence wavered for a moment.

"If you will ask her to come to me here, perhaps between us we may persuade her," he said in his most ingratiating manner.

"She is not here."

"I see. When do you expect her to return?"

Instead of answering him, Mrs. Coomb stuck her nose in the air and abruptly left him.

Perplexed, Andreas looked after her.

Mr. Langtry shook his head.

"It is just as well, old boy. You are about to botch the business royally."

"I do not need your advice on how to court a woman," Andreas snapped.

"Oh, I think you do." His tone was irritatingly superior.

Andreas cast a haughty eye over Mr. Langtry's unprepossessing appearance. His brown coat was tailored by a craftsman of the highest order—at least two years ago. His boots, though of excellent quality, were scuffed and well worn.

Mr. Langtry, instead of being intimidated by this scrutiny, burst into laughter.

"Have you never wondered why Madelyn preferred me to you?"

Every day for the past year and a half.

"A temporary attack of brain fever?" suggested Andreas with an arch smile instead.

"Good guess," Mr. Langtry acknowledged with a glimmer of amusement. "But no. It is because I came to her with nothing but my heart to lay at her feet."

"And four adorable children who looked at her with worship in their eyes," Andreas scoffed. "You did not fight fair, Mr. Langtry. You left the woman with no choice."

"Did I?"

Andreas gave a snort of derision.

"You *know* you did! Here was I, ready to offer her my five-hundred-year-old name and make her the mistress of my palace and villa in the most romantic city in the world, but you—" He stopped abruptly and stared in sudden comprehension.

"You were saying?" prompted Mr. Langtry.

"Offered nothing but yourself," the count said slowly.

Mr. Langtry pantomimed applause.

"With abject humility," Mr. Langtry said. "Do not forget that part."

"I have not," Andreas said, suddenly ashamed of the glittering gold casket, the fragrant sandalwood, the tokens of wealth he had chosen to dazzle Amelia and impress her mother. "But am I to go to her with nothing?"

"Well, maybe a little something," Mr. Langtry conceded. "I had the adorable children after all. Let us see what you have in the pretty box."

He gave a vulgar whistle when he withdrew the long rope of matched pearls.

"They are from the Orient," Andreas said.

"And worth a king's ransom, I have no doubt," Mr. Langtry said admiringly. He next withdrew a stunning brooch of rubies set in antique gold.

"Fifteenth century, of Florentine workmanship," Andreas explained. "It belonged to the Medicis."

"Now, this would become Madelyn," Mr. Langtry said when he reverently withdrew a collar of emeralds and diamonds set in gold.

"So I thought when I ordered it made for her," Andreas said dryly. "I had thought to present it to her on our wedding night, but since that was not meant to be, I thought Amelia might like it."

"Subtle, aren't you?" Mr. Langtry said with a shake of his head as he put it back in the casket. He continued pawing through the little chest. "I don't suppose you had the time to have some other ostentatious trinket made up for Miss Coomb—" Suddenly his attention was arrested, and his brows drew together. "Hallo! What is this?"

He withdrew his hand and held out a dainty band of gold carved in a rose pattern with a large oval aquamarine at its center.

Andreas shrugged his shoulders.

"I bought it in one of the shops on the Rialto Bridge because the stone matches her eyes exactly. I could not resist it, although the quality is not of the very best. It was, as you say, an impulse."

"The very thing," Mr. Langtry declared.

"Just this? This . . . *nothing?*" Andreas sputtered in astonishment. The ring looked tiny and insignificant on Langtry's large palm. "I cannot give her this alone!"

"Why not?"

"How can you ask? It is unworthy of—"

Mr. Langtry regarded him with raised eyebrows.

"Me," Andreas admitted. "I was about to say this

trifle is unworthy of her, but I meant that it is unworthy of me."

"I do believe there is hope for you yet, old man," Mr. Langtry said approvingly.

He tossed the ring to Andreas, and he caught it in midair.

"There you go, then," Langtry said. "Godspeed and all that."

He sketched a mocking benediction in the air with his right hand and turned away.

"But I do not know where to find her," the count objected. A sudden terrible thought struck him. "She has not gone back to England?"

"And if she has?"

"I will follow her! At once!"

"Excellent," Mr. Langtry said. "Happily, she is a bit closer to hand than that.

"Oh, Miss Coomb," Miss Lorimar said in rapture as she scrambled over the large, picturesque rocks that formed the bed of a freshwater river that flowed with a musical murmur down a hill and emptied into Ermones Bay on the island of Corfu's west coast. She indicated the blindingly blue waters of the Ionian Sea that kissed a sandy beach. "It is even lovelier than I imagined! This is the very spot where the hero Odysseus first beheld the princess Nausicaa. I just know it."

Amelia smiled at her friend, who was an enthusiastic admirer of Homer and other tellers of ancient tales, and she was glad she had succeeded in making *someone* happy. Nearby, Amelia's maid unhurriedly gathered the remains of their picnic from the wildflower-strewn lush green grass.

In truth, it had been a good idea to come to Corfu,

although it had cost Amelia some heartsickness to leave Venice.

He did not want her.

He did not need her.

She would bring him nothing but disgrace if he submitted to her mother's coercion to offer her marriage and thus save her besmirched reputation.

Indeed, she was exceedingly grateful to Miss Lorimar, for she was the only one of Amelia's acquaintances in Venice who had been willing to receive her in her disgrace.

She suspected that Miss Lorimar's presence on this pleasure trip cost her a furious scold from her sister-in-law, who was very high in the instep and was, moreover, reluctant to lose the services of Miss Lorimar as an unpaid dogsbody while she toured Corfu at Amelia's invitation.

Amelia took a deep breath of the salt-scented air and turned her face up to the sun.

No need to protect her complexion from freckles, she thought wryly, now that she was an outcast from society.

Incredibly, for the first time in weeks, her troubled heart almost felt at peace.

The sound of stone being dislodged made her turn around quickly and look straight into *his* eyes.

Was she dreaming? She blinked, but the apparition had not dissolved.

"Andreas?" she asked in disbelief.

He wore no coat, for it was a hot day, and his shirt-sleeves billowed in the breeze that tossed his golden curls. He carried some wildflowers in his hand.

He knelt at her feet and offered them to her.

"Er, thank you," she whispered, ashamed of the juice of ripe blackberries that still stained her hands from their picnic. She would have hidden them behind her back, but he reached out and grabbed one. He kissed it, then smiled and tasted the tip of one of her fingers.

"Your skin is as sweet as I remember," the count declared. He lowered his voice to an intimate whisper. "I adore the way you blush when I touch you, *carissima*. I must have you. Will you be mine?"

She averted her face in embarrassment.

"You are not asking me to be your mistress, are you? Because if you are, I—"

"Would you accept?" he interrupted.

Her basilisk stare gave him his answer.

"I thought not," he said with a soft laugh. "Forgive me for teasing you, beloved. I am very bad at this, for I have had little practice in asking ladies to marry me."

"Has my mother forced you to this?" she asked. "I have told her—"

He stood and placed the tips of his fingers to her lips.

"Peace, my love. Your mother has nothing to do with my presence here."

"But, the disgrace—I am not received anywhere, you know."

"What is that to us? You have sacrificed your reputation for my sake. Do you think I care the snap of my fingers for the chattering of idle tongues? As my wife, you will be received everywhere. Do you doubt it?"

"You think you are obligated to marry me out of gratitude. Well, I will not have it! I will *not* be reduced to begging for a husband!"

"It is I who will do the begging," he said. "Please. Be my wife."

She smiled sadly at him.

"No, Andreas. It is kind of you to offer, but I cannot

accept—" She blinked in surprise when Andreas grasped her hands and shook his head to silence her. He made a gesture to his left, and Amelia beheld Miss Lorimar, whose existence she had quite forgotten.

"Oh, pardon me," exclaimed Miss Lorimar, who had come to see who was talking to her friend and was brought up short with a gasp when she realized that she had unwittingly interrupted an intimate scene.

Andreas gave her a dazzling smile.

"I do not believe we have met, Miss—?

Since Miss Lorimar had been robbed of speech, Amelia stepped into the breech.

"Count Briccetti, may I introduce my friend Miss Lorimar?"

"Charmed, Miss Lorimar," the count said with a regal inclination of his head.

"Me too. Charmed. That is, I will wait for Miss Coomb over there." The flustered young woman made a distracted gesture toward the beach. "Carry on."

She backed away and almost tripped over a rock in her haste to give them privacy.

Andreas smiled down into Amelia's eyes.

"I believe you were saying how *kind* it is of me to offer for you," he reminded her as he stroked her jaw with the back of his knuckles. She trembled. "Such delicious skin," he added as he cupped her face in his hands and bent to kiss her. "Such a beautiful, tender mouth."

"You do not *want* to marry me," she managed to say.

"Do I not?" he said just before he captured her lips.

He made a thorough job of it. When he finished kissing her, he clasped her against his chest, which was just as well, because her knees had turned to jelly. She could feel the rapid, urgent drumbeat of his heart against the side of her face.

He was not so confident of her answer as he seemed.

She looked up at him in surprise to see ~~real anxiety~~ in his eyes.

"*Carissima,* I have failed my country. I tell myself I do not deserve you."

"Oh, Andreas. That is not true—"

"Then I have to ask myself," he said with a glimmer of his old arrogance. "Who can make Amelia more happy than Andreas? And the answer is no one," he murmured as his lips brushed hers. "So I come to you in all humility to throw myself at your feet. You will accept, yes?"

She had to laugh at that.

"Oh, well, as long as you are being *humble!*"

"I am most humble," he said earnestly. "I have brought you only this insignificant bauble." He withdrew a small blue velvet bag from his pocket and untied the silver cord that secured it. He emptied it into his palm and regarded it with uncertainty.

"It is unworthy," he pronounced as he closed his fingers over it. "To give you this thing is to insult us both."

"Perhaps you could let me decide for myself," she said as she held her open hand under his fist.

He shrugged and dropped the jewel into her hand. He looked away.

It was a gold ring set with a large aquamarine.

"I bought it in one of the shops on the Rialto Bridge," he said. "It reminded me of your eyes, and I had to buy it for you. Today I see it does not do your eyes justice."

"It is perfect!" she cried. "I have never seen anything so beautiful."

He took the ring from her hand and placed it on her finger.

"Your answer is yes, then?" he asked.

"Yes!" She put her arms around his neck and drew his face down to hers so she could cover his jaw with ardent little kisses. "Yes, and yes, and yes, and yes!" Because she could not bear to take her eyes off either the ring or his face, she held up her hand behind him to admire the way the Ionian sunlight played along the jewel's facets.

"To think I have won you with so little," he said. His eyes were alight with affectionate amusement. "This humility is a very good thing. Would you like to be married here, on this beach? With only the seabirds and a priest to witness our joy?"

"That would be wildly romantic," she said pensively. "But no."

"No?" he asked, brows knit.

"I think," she said, "that you have been humble enough."

He grinned.

"We will make those who snubbed you eat their words, yes?"

"Oh, yes," she said as she snuggled under his arm and beckoned to Miss Lorimar so she could be the first to share their joy.

Eighteen

"Peach brocade," Robert Langtry said with a snort of scornful amusement as he and Lady Madelyn stepped out of the flower-decked gondola. "Was there ever such a fellow?"

Madelyn smiled at Count Andreas Briccetti, resplendent in peach brocade and with a diamond the size of a hen's egg winking from the fold of his snowy cravat. He bowed to her and winked.

"No," she said dreamily. "I don't think there ever was."

She stumbled and would have ended up in the canal if her husband hadn't caught her.

Lady Madelyn laughed at his disgruntled expression.

"Regrets?" he asked.

"None whatsoever," she said with a grin. "You must admit, though, that when the count means to make a statement, he does so by no half-measures."

Robert did not answer right away because he had to help an ecstatic Mrs. Coomb from the boat.

"Oh, the darling man," Mrs. Coomb said as she gave her future son-in-law a flirtatious wave of her lace-gloved hand. He rewarded her with a dazzling smile.

It was hard to believe that a month ago he had been

a vile seducer and a base deceiver. Apparently all was forgiven in her daughter's triumph.

The same society that had snubbed Miss Coomb a short time ago had spent the days leading to the wedding flattering her mother in hope of receiving invitations to a celebration that promised to be the most exclusive of the season.

A burst of applause from the crowds lining the Grand Canal greeted the arrival of the extravagantly flower-garlanded bridal gondola, and Andreas turned shining eyes toward the sound.

Every young lady in Venetian society had called on Amelia in the hopes of being asked to form one of her court of bridesmaids, but Miss Lorimar, dressed in a becoming gown of pink tiffany and creamy lace, was the only one chosen for this honor.

It had gone a long way to pacifying her sister-in-law, who had been horrified by Miss Lorimar's refusal to snub Amelia during the period of her disgrace.

As for the bride herself, she sat in a thronelike gilded chair at the middle of the gondola, like a queen.

Her exquisite off-the-shoulder white brocade gown was embroidered with golden thread and crystal beads. A gold circlet set with diamonds adorned her brow and held the filmy panel of sheer silk that formed her veil and trailed over the back of her shoulders. Her golden hair flowed to her waist, and she carried a bouquet of peach and yellow roses from the greenhouse at the count's villa.

"Bellissima," the count whispered into her ear as he helped her out of the gondola. He kissed her hand, and the crowd lining the canal sent up a cheer.

Hand in hand, the couple walked the short distance to the Piazza San Marco as the crowd paced along with them at a respectful distance.

The very bronze chariot horses atop the archway to

St. Mark's Basilica wore collars of rosettes and trailing ribbons.

"How absurd!" Amelia exclaimed on a gurgle of laughter when she saw them. "Is it any wonder that I adore you?"

"No, it is not," the count said modestly.

ABOUT THE AUTHOR

KATE HUNTINGTON lives with her family in Illinois. She is the author of six Zebra Regency romances and is currently working on her seventh, which will be published in 2003. Kate loves hearing from readers, and you may write to her c/o Zebra Books. Please include a self-addressed stamped envelope if you wish a reply.

Discover The Magic of
Romance With

Jo Goodman

__More Than You Know $5.99US/$7.99CAN
  0-8217-6569-8

__Crystal Passion $5.99US/$7.50CAN
  0-8217-6308-3

__Always in My Dreams $5.50US/$7.00CAN
  0-8217-5619-2

__The Captain's Lady $5.99US/$7.50CAN
  0-8217-5948-5

__Seaswept Abandon $5.99US/$7.99CAN
  0-8217-6709-7

__Only in My Arms $5.99US/$7.50CAN
  0-8217-5346-0

Call toll free **1-888-345-BOOK** to order by phone or use this coupon
to order by mail, or order online at **www.kensingtonbooks.com**.
Name_____
Address_____
City_____ State _____ Zip _____
Please send me the books that I have checked above.
I am enclosing $_____
Plus postage and handling* $_____
Sales tax (in New York and Tennessee) $_____
Total amount enclosed $_____
*Add $2.50 for the first book and $.50 for each additional book. Send
check or money order (no cash or CODs) to:
Kensington Publishing Corp., 850 Third Avenue, New York, NY 10022
Prices and numbers subject to change without notice.
All orders subject to availability.
Check out our website at **www.kensingtonbooks.com**.

DO YOU HAVE THE
HOHL COLLECTION?

__Another Spring $6.99US/$8.99CAN
   0-8217-7155-8

__Compromises $6.99US/$8.99CAN
   0-8217-7154-X

__Ever After $6.99US/$8.99CAN
   0-8217-7203-1

__Something Special $5.99US/$7.50CAN
   0-8217-6725-9

__Maybe Tomorrow $6.99US/$7.99CAN
   0-8217-7349-6

__My Own $6.99US/$8.99CAN
   0-8217-6640-6

__Never Say Never $5.99US/$7.99CAN
   0-8217-6379-2

__Silver Thunder $6.99US/$8.99CAN
   0-8217-7201-5

Call toll free **1-888-345-BOOK** to order by phone or use this coupon
to order by mail. ALL BOOKS AVAILABLE DECEMBER 1, 2000.
Name_____
Address_____
City_____ State _____ Zip _____
Please send me the books that I have checked above.
I am enclosing $_____
Plus postage and handling* $_____
Sales tax (in New York and Tennessee) $_____
Total amount enclosed $_____
*Add $2.50 for the first book and $.50 for each additional book. Send check
or money order (no cash or CODs) to:
Kensington Publishing Corp., 850 Third Avenue, New York, NY 10022
Prices and numbers subject to change without notice. Valid only in the U.S.
All orders subject to availability. **NO ADVANCE ORDERS.**
Visit out our website at **www.kensingtonbooks.com**.

Embrace the Romances of

Shannon Drake

__Come the Morning $6.99US/$8.99CAN
0-8217-6471-3

__Blue Heaven, Black Night $6.50US/$8.00CAN
0-8217-5982-5

__Conquer the Night $6.99US/$8.99CAN
0-8217-6639-2

__The King's Pleasure $6.50US/$8.00CAN
0-8217-5857-8

__Lie Down in Roses $5.99US/$6.99CAN
0-8217-4749-0

__Tomorrow the Glory $5.99US/$6.99CAN
0-7860-0021-4

Call toll free **1-888-345-BOOK** to order by phone or use this coupon to order by mail.

Name_____

Address_____

City_____ State _____ Zip _____

Please send me the books that I have checked above.

I am enclosing $_____
Plus postage and handling* $_____
Sales tax (in New York and Tennessee) $_____
Total amount enclosed $_____

*Add $2.50 for the first book and $.50 for each additional book. Send check or money order (no cash or CODs) to:
Kensington Publishing Corp., 850 Third Avenue, New York, NY 10022
Prices and numbers subject to change without notice.
All orders subject to availability.
Check out our website at **www.kensingtonbooks.com**.

Discover The Magic Of
Romance With

Janis Reams Hudson

__**Apache Magic**
0-8217-6186-2   **$5.99US/$7.50CAN**

__**Apache Promise**
0-8217-6451-9   **$5.99US/$7.99CAN**

__**Hunter's Touch**
0-8217-6344-X   **$5.99US/$7.99CAN**

__**Long Way Home**
0-8217-6923-5   **$5.99US/$7.99CAN**

Call toll free **1-888-345-BOOK** to order by phone or use
this coupon to order by mail.
Name_____
 Address_____
City_____ State_____ Zip_____
Please send me the books I have checked above.
I am enclosing $_____
Plus postage and handling* $_____
Sales tax (in New York and Tennessee only) $_____
Total amount enclosed $_____
*Add $2.50 for the first book and $.50 for each additional book.
Send check or money order (no cash or CODs) to: **Kensington Publishing
Corp., Dept. C.O., 850 Third Avenue, Floor, New York, NY 10022**
Prices and numbers subject to change without notice. All orders subject
to availability. Visit our website at **www.kensingtonbooks.com**

More Zebra Regency Romances

__A Taste for Love by Donna Bell $4.99US/$6.50CAN
    0-8217-6104-8

__An Unlikely Father by Lynn Collum $4.99US/$6.99CAN
    0-8217-6418-7

__An Unexpected Husband by Jo Ann Ferguson $4.99US/$6.99CAN
    0-8217-6481-0

__Wedding Ghost by Cindy Holbrook $4.99US/$6.50CAN
    0-8217-6217-6

__Lady Diana's Darlings by Kate Huntington $4.99US/$6.99CAN
    0-8217-6655-4

__A London Flirtation by Valerie King $4.99US/$6.99CAN
    0-8217-6535-3

__Lord Langdon's Tutor by Laura Paquet $4.99US/$6.99CAN
    0-8217-6675-9

__Lord Mumford's Minx by Debbie Raleigh $4.99US/$6.99CAN
    0-8217-6673-2

__Lady Serena's Surrender by Jeanne Savery $4.99US/$6.99CAN
    0-8217-6607-4

__A Dangerous Dalliance by Regina Scott $4.99US/$6.99CAN
    0-8217-6609-0

__Lady May's Folly by Donna Simpson $4.99US/$6.99CAN
    0-8217-6805-0

Call toll free **1-888-345-BOOK** to order by phone or use this coupon to order by mail.

Name_____

Address_____

City_____ State_____ Zip_____

Please send me the books I have checked above.

I am enclosing $_____

Plus postage and handling* $_____

Sales tax (in New York and Tennessee only) $_____

Total amount enclosed $_____

*Add $2.50 for the first book and $.50 for each additional book.

Send check or money order (no cash or CODs) to:

Kensington Publishing Corp., 850 Third Avenue, New York, NY 10022

Prices and numbers subject to change without notice.

All orders subject to availability.

Check out our website at **www.kensingtonbooks.com**.